# THE THIRD MAN
## and
# THE FALLEN IDOL

This volume contains the original versions of Graham Greene's stories *The Third Man* and *The Fallen Idol*, both of which were made into memorable and outstandingly successful films. *The Third Man* is the story of a writer's attempts to clear the name of his dead friend, Harry Lime, a racketeer in the underworld of post-war Vienna. *The Fallen Idol* tells of a small boy left in a large house in Belgravia with his hero, the butler, and the butler's jealous, waspish wife.

# THE THIRD MAN
## and
# THE FALLEN IDOL

## Graham Greene

**CURLEY LARGE PRINT**
HAMPTON, NEW HAMPSHIRE

**Library of Congress Cataloging-in-Publication Data**

Greene, Graham, 1904–
  [Third man]
  The third man; and, The fallen idol / Graham Greene.
    p.  cm.
  ISBN  0–7927–1909–3
  ISBN  0–7927–1908–5 (pbk.)
  1. Large type books.  I. Greene, Graham, 1904–  Fallen idol.
1994.  II. Title.
  [PR6013.R44T5  1994]
  823'.912—dc20                                        93–39312
                                                            CIP

---

**British Library Cataloguing in Publication Data available**

This Large Print edition is published by Chivers Press, England, and by
Curley Large Print, an imprint of Chivers North America, 1994.


U.K. Hardcover  ISBN  0  7451  2132  2
U.K. Softcover   ISBN  0  7451  2144  6
U.S. Hardcover  ISBN  0  7927  1909  3
U.S. Softcover   ISBN  0  7927  1908  5

*Printed in Great Britain*

To Carol Reed
in admiration and affection
and in memory of so many early morning
Vienna hours at Maxim's, the Casanova, the
Oriental

# PREFACE

*The Third Man* was never written to be read but only to be seen. Like many love affairs it started at a dinner table and continued with many headaches in many places: Vienna, Venice, Ravello, London, Santa Monica.

Most novelists, I suppose, carry round in their heads or in their notebooks the first ideas for stories that have never come to be written. Sometimes one turns them over after many years and thinks regretfully that they would have been good once, in a time now dead. So years back, on the flap of an envelope I had written an opening paragraph: 'I had paid my last farewell to Harry a week ago, when his coffin was lowered into the frozen February ground, so that it was with incredulity that I saw him pass by, without a sign of recognition, among the host of strangers in the Strand.' I, no more than my hero, had pursued Harry, so when Sir Alexander Korda asked me to write a film for Carol Reed—to follow our *Fallen Idol*—I had nothing more to offer than this paragraph. Though Korda wanted a film about the four-power occupation of Vienna, he was prepared to let me pursue the tracks of Harry Lime.

To me it is almost impossible to write a film play without first writing a story. Even a film depends on more than plot, on a certain measure of characterisation, on mood and atmosphere; and these seem to me almost impossible to capture for the first time in the dull shorthand of a script. One can reproduce an effect caught in another medium, but one cannot make the first act of creation in script form. One must have the sense of more material than one needs to draw on. *The Third Man*, therefore, though never intended for publication, had to start as a story before those apparently interminable transformations from one treatment to another.

On these treatments Carol Reed and I worked closely together, covering so many feet of carpet a day, acting scenes at each other. No third ever joined our conferences; so much value lies in the clear cut-and-thrust of argument between two people. To the novelist, of course, his novel is the best he can do with a particular subject; he cannot help resenting many of the changes necessary for turning it into a film or a play; but *The Third Man* was never intended to be more than the raw material for a picture. The reader will notice many differences between the story and the film, and he should not imagine these changes were forced on an unwilling author: as likely as not they were suggested by the author. The film, in fact, is better than the story because it is in this case the finished state of the story.

Some of these changes have obvious superficial reasons. The choice of an American instead of an English star involved a number of alterations. For example, Mr. Joseph Cotten quite reasonably objected to the name Rollo. The name had to be an absurd one, and the name Holley occurred to me when I remembered that figure of fun, the American poet Thomas Holley Chivers. An American, too, could hardly have been mistaken for the great English writer Dexter, whose literary character bore certain echoes of the gentle genius of Mr. E. M. Forster. The confusion of identities would have been impossible, even if Carol Reed had not rightly objected to a rather far-fetched situation involving a great deal of explanation that increased the length of a film already far too long. Another minor point: in deference to American opinion a Rumanian was substituted for Cooler, since Mr. Orson Welles' engagement had already supplied us with one American villain. (Incidentally, the popular line of dialogue concerning Swiss cuckoo clocks was written into the script by Mr. Welles himself.)

One of the very few major disputes between Carol Reed and myself concerned the ending, and he has been proved triumphantly right. I held the view that an entertainment of this kind was too light an affair to carry the weight of an unhappy ending. Reed on his side felt that my ending—indeterminate though it was, with no words spoken—would strike the audience, who had just seen Harry die, as unpleasantly cynical. I admit I was only half convinced; I was afraid few people would wait in their seats during the girl's long walk from the graveside and that they would leave the cinema under the impression that the ending was as conventional as mine and more drawn-out. I had not given enough consideration to the mastery of Reed's direction, and at that stage, of course, we neither of us could have anticipated Reed's brilliant discovery of Mr. Karas, the zither player.

The episode of the Russians kidnapping Anna (a perfectly possible incident in Vienna) was eliminated at a fairly late stage. It was not satisfactorily tied into the story, and it threatened to turn the film into a propagandist picture. We had no desire to move people's political emotions; we wanted to entertain them, to frighten them a little, to make them laugh.

Reality, in fact, was only a background to a fairy tale; nonetheless the story of the penicillin racket is based on a truth all the more grim because so many of the agents were more innocent than Joseph Harbin. The other day in London a surgeon took two friends to see the film. He was surprised to find them subdued and depressed by a picture he had enjoyed. They then told him that at the end of the war when they were with the Royal Air Force they had themselves sold penicillin in Vienna. The possible consequences of their act had never before occurred to them.

# CHAPTER ONE

ONE never knows when the blow may fall. When I saw Rollo Martins first I made this note on him for my security police files: 'In normal circumstances a cheerful fool. Drinks too much and may cause a little trouble. Whenever a woman passes raises his eyes and makes some comment, but I get the impression that really he'd rather not be bothered. Has never really grown up and perhaps that accounts for the way he worshipped Lime.' I wrote there that phrase 'in normal circumstances' because I met him first at Harry Lime's funeral. It was February, and the gravediggers had been forced to use electric drills to open the frozen ground in Vienna's Central Cemetery. It was as if even nature were doing its best to reject Lime, but we got him in at last and laid the earth back on him like bricks. He was vaulted in, and Rollo Martins walked quickly away as though his long gangly legs wanted to break into a run, and the tears of a boy ran down his thirty-five-year-old face. Rollo Martins believed in friendship, and that was why what happened later was a worse shock to him than it would have been to you or me (you because you would have put it down to an illusion and me because at once a rational explanation—however wrongly—would have come to my mind). If only he had come to tell me then, what a lot of trouble would have been saved.

If you are to understand this strange, rather sad story you must have an impression at least of the background—the smashed dreary city of Vienna divided up in zones among the four powers; the Russian, the British, the American, the French zones, regions marked only by notice boards, and in the centre of the city, surrounded by the Ring with its heavy public buildings and its prancing statuary, the Inner Stadt under the control of all four powers. In this once fashionable Inner Stadt each power in turn, for a month at a time, takes, as we call it, 'the chair', and becomes responsible for security; at night, if you were fool enough to waste your Austrian schillings on a night club, you would be fairly certain to see the International Power at work—four military police, one from each power, communicating with each other, if they communicated at all, in the common language of their enemy. I never knew Vienna between the wars, and I am too young to remember the old Vienna with its Strauss music and its bogus easy charm; to me it is simply a city of undignified ruins which turned that February into great glaciers of snow and ice. The Danube was a grey flat muddy river a long way off across the second Bezirk, the Russian zone where the Prater lay smashed and desolate and full of weeds, only the Great Wheel revolving slowly over the foundations of merry-go-rounds like abandoned millstones, the rusting iron of smashed tanks which nobody had cleared away, the frost-nipped weeds where the snow was thin. I haven't enough imagination to picture it as it had once been, any more than I can picture Sacher's Hotel as other than a transit hotel for English officers or see the Kärntnerstrasse as a fashionable shopping street instead of a street which exists, most of it, only at eye level, repaired up to the first storey. A Russian soldier in a fur cap goes by with a rifle over his shoulder, a few tarts cluster round the American Information Office and men in overcoats sip ersatz coffee in the windows of the Old Vienna. At night it is just as well to stick to the Inner Stadt or the zones of three of the powers, though even there the kidnappings occur—such senseless kidnappings they sometimes

3

seemed to us—a Ukrainian girl without a passport, an old man beyond the age of usefulness, sometimes of course the technician or traitor. This was roughly the Vienna to which Rollo Martins came on February seventh last year. I have reconstructed the affair as best I can from my own files and from what Martins told me. It is as accurate as I can make it—I haven't invented a line of dialogue, though I can't vouch for Martins' memory; an ugly story if you leave out the girl: grim and sad and unrelieved if it were not for that absurd episode of the British Cultural Relations Society lecturer.

# CHAPTER TWO

A BRITISH subject can still travel if he is content to take with him only five English pounds which he is forbidden to spend abroad, but if Rollo Martins had not received an invitation from Lime of the International Refugee Office he would not have been allowed to enter Austria, which counts still as occupied territory. Lime had suggested that Martins might write up the business of looking after the international refugees, and although it wasn't Martins' usual line, he had consented. It would give him a holiday, and he badly needed a holiday after the incident in Dublin and the other incident in Amsterdam; he always tried to dismiss women as 'incidents', things that simply happened to him without any will of his own, acts of God in the eyes of insurance agents. He had a haggard look when he arrived in Vienna and a habit of looking over his shoulder that for a time made me suspicious of him until I realised that he went in fear that one of, say, six people might turn up unexpectedly. He told me vaguely that he had been mixing his drinks—that was another way of putting it.

5

Rollo Martins' usual line was the writing of cheap paper-covered Westerns under the name of Buck Dexter. His public was large but unremunerative. He couldn't have afforded Vienna if Lime had not offered to pay his expenses when he got there out of some vaguely described propaganda fund. Lime could also, he said, keep him supplied with paper bafs—the only currency in use from a penny upwards in British hotels and clubs. So it was with exactly five unusable pound notes that Martins arrived in Vienna.

An odd incident had occurred at Frankfurt, where the plane from London grounded for an hour. Martins was eating a hamburger in the American canteen (a kindly airline supplied the passengers with a voucher for sixty-five cents' worth of food) when a man he could recognise from twenty feet away as a journalist approached his table.

'You Mr. Dexter?' he asked.

'Yes,' Martins said, taken off his guard.

'You look younger than your photographs,' the man said. 'Like to make a statement? I represent the local forces paper here. We'd like to know what you think of Frankfurt.'

'I only touched down ten minutes ago.'

'Fair enough,' the man said. 'What about views on the American novel?'

'I don't read them,' Martins said.

'The well-known acid-humour,' the journalist said. He pointed at a small grey-haired man with protruding teeth, nibbling a bit of bread. 'Happen to know if that's Carey?'

'No. What Carey?'

'J. G. Carey of course.'

'I've never heard of him.'

'You novelists live out of the world. He's my real assignment,' and Martins watched him make across the room for the great Carey, who greeted him with a false headline smile, laying down his crust. Dexter wasn't the man's assignment, but Martins couldn't help feeling a certain pride—nobody had ever before referred to him as a novelist; and that sense of pride and importance carried him over the disappointment when Lime was not there to meet him at the airport. We never get accustomed to being less important to other people than they are to us—Martins felt the little jab of dispensability, standing by the bus door, watching the snow come sifting down, so thinly and softly that the great drifts among the ruined buildings had an air of permanence, as though they were not the result of this meagre fall, but lay, for ever, above the line of perpetual snow.

There was no Lime to meet him at the Hotel Astoria, where the bus landed him, and no message—only a cryptic one for Mr. Dexter from someone he had never heard of called Crabbin. 'We expected you on tomorrow's plane. Please stay where you are. On the way round. Hotel room booked.' But Rollo Martins wasn't the kind of man who stayed around. If you stayed around in a hotel lounge, sooner or later incidents occurred; one mixed one's drinks. I can hear Rollo Martins saying to me, 'I've done with incidents. No more incidents,' before he plunged head first into the most serious incident of all. There was always a conflict in Rollo Martins—between the absurd Christian name and the sturdy Dutch (four generations back) surname. Rollo looked at every woman that passed, and Martins renounced them for ever. I don't know which one of them wrote the Westerns.

Martins had been given Lime's address and he felt no curiosity about the man called Crabbin; it was too obvious that a mistake had been made, though he didn't yet connect it with the conversation at Frankfurt. Lime had written that he could put Martins up in his own flat, a large apartment on the edge of Vienna that had been requisitioned from a

Nazi owner. Lime could pay for the taxi when he arrived, so Martins drove straight away to the building lying in the third (British) zone. He kept the taxi waiting while he mounted to the third floor.

How quickly one becomes aware of silence even in so silent a city as Vienna with the snow steadily settling. Martins hadn't reached the second floor before he was convinced that he would not find Lime there, but the silence was deeper than just absence—it was as if he would not find Lime anywhere in Vienna, and, as he reached the third floor and saw the big black bow over the door handle, anywhere in the world at all. Of course it might have been a cook who had died, a housekeeper, anybody but Harry Lime, but he knew—he felt he had known twenty stairs down—that Lime, the Lime he had hero-worshipped now for twenty years, since the first meeting in a grim school corridor with a cracked bell ringing for prayers, was gone. Martins wasn't wrong, not entirely wrong. After he had rung the bell half a dozen times a small man with a sullen expression put his head out from another flat and told him in a tone of vexation, 'It's no use. There's nobody there. He's dead.'

'Herr Lime?'

'Herr Lime of course.'

Martins said to me later, 'At first it didn't mean a thing. It was just a bit of information, like those paragraphs in *The Times* they call "News in Brief". I said to him, "When did it happen? How?"'

'He was run over by a car,' the man said. 'Last Thursday,' He added sullenly, as if really this were none of his business, 'They're burying him this afternoon. You've only just missed them.'

'Them?'

'Oh, a couple of friends and the coffin.'

'Wasn't he in hospital?'

'There was no sense in taking him to hospital. He was killed here on his own doorstep— instantaneously. The right-hand mudguard struck him on his shoulder and bowled him over like a rabbit.'

It was only then, Martins told me, when the man used the word 'rabbit', that the dead Harry Lime came alive, became the boy with the gun which he had shown Martins the means of 'borrowing'; a boy starting up among the long sandy burrows of Brickworth Common saying, 'Shoot, you fool, shoot! There,' and the rabbit limped to cover, wounded by Martins' shot.

'Where are they burying him?' he asked the

10

stranger on the landing.

'In the Central Cemetery. They'll have a hard time of it in this frost.'

He had no idea how to pay for his taxi, or indeed where in Vienna he could find a room in which he could live for five English pounds, but that problem had to be postponed until he had seen the last of Harry Lime. He drove straight out of town into the suburb (British zone) where the Central Cemetery lay. One passed through the Russian zone to reach it, and took a short cut through the American zone, which you couldn't mistake because of the ice-cream parlours in every street. The trams ran along the high wall of the Central Cemetery, and for a mile on the other side of the rails stretched the monumental masons and the market gardeners—an apparently endless chain of gravestones waiting for owners and wreaths waiting for mourners.

Martins had not realised the size of this huge snowbound park where he was making his last rendezvous with Lime. It was as if Harry had left a message to him, 'Meet me in Hyde Park,' without specifying a spot between the Achilles statue and Lancaster Gate; the avenues of graves, each avenue numbered and lettered, stretched out like the spokes of an enormous wheel; they drove for a half-mile towards the west, and then turned and drove a half-mile north, turned south. . . . The snow gave the great pompous family headstones an air of grotesque comedy; a toupee of snow slipped sidesway over an angelic face, a saint wore a heavy white moustache, and a shako of snow tipped at a drunken angle over the bust of a superior civil servant called Wolfgang Gottmann. Even this cemetery was zoned between the powers: the Russian zone was marked by huge tasteless statues of armed men, the French by rows of anonymous wooden crosses and a torn tired tricolour flag. Then Martins remembered that Lime was a Catholic and was unlikely to be buried in the British zone for which they had been vainly searching. So back they drove through the heart of a forest where the graves lay like wolves under the trees, winking white eyes under the gloom of the evergreens. Once from under the trees emerged a group of three men in strange eighteenth-century black and silver uniforms with three-cornered hats pushing a kind of barrow: they crossed a ride in the forest of graves and disappeared again.

It was just chance that they found the funeral in time—one patch in the enormous park where the snow had been shovelled aside and a tiny group was gathered, apparently bent on some very private business. A priest had finished speaking, his words coming secretively through the thin patient snow, and a coffin was on the point of being lowered into the ground. Two men in lounge suits stood at the graveside; one carried a wreath that he obviously had forgotten to drop on to the coffin, for his companion nudged his elbow so that he came to with a start and dropped the flowers. A girl stood a little way away with her hands over her face, and I stood twenty yards away by another grave, watching with relief the last of Lime and noticing carefully who was there—just a man in a mackintosh I was to Martins. He came up to me and said, 'Could you tell me who they are burying?'

'A fellow called Lime,' I said, and was astonished to see the tears start to this stranger's eyes: he didn't look like a man who wept, nor was Lime the kind of man whom I thought likely to have mourners—genuine mourners with genuine tears. There was the girl of course, but one excepts women from all such generalisations.

Martins stood there, till the end, close beside me. He said to me later that as an old friend he didn't want to intrude on these newer ones—Lime's death belonged to them, let them have it. He was under the

sentimental illusion that Lime's life—
twenty years of it anyway—belonged to him.
As soon as the affair was over—I am not a religious man and always feel a little impatient
with the fuss that surrounds death—Martins
strode away on his long legs that always
seemed likely to get entangled together, back
to his taxi. He made no attempt to speak to
anyone, and the tears now were really running, at any rate the few meagre drops that
any of us can squeeze out at our age.

One's file, you know, is never quite complete; a case is never really closed, even after a
century, when all the participants are dead.
So I followed Martins: I knew the other three:
I wanted to know the stranger. I caught him
up by his taxi and said, 'I haven't any transport. Would you give me a lift into town?'

'Of course,' he said. I knew the driver of my
jeep would spot me as we came out and follow
us unobtrusively. As we drove away I noticed
he never looked behind—it's nearly always
the fake mourners and the fake lovers who
take that last look, who wait waving on plat-
forms, instead of clearing quickly out, not
looking back. Is it perhaps that they love
themselves so much and want to keep themselves in the sight of others, even of the dead?

I said, 'My name's Calloway.'

'Martins,' he said.

'You were a friend of Lime?'

'Yes.' Most people in the last week would have hesitated before they admitted quite so much.

'Been here long?'

'I only came this afternoon from England. Harry had asked me to stay with him. I hadn't heard.'

'Bit of a shock?'

'Look here,' he said, 'I badly want a drink, but I haven't any cash—except five pounds sterling. I'd be awfully grateful if you'd stand me one.'

It was my turn to say 'Of course'. I thought for a moment and told the driver the name of a small bar in the Kärntnerstrasse. I didn't think he'd want to be seen for a while in a busy British bar full of transit officers and their wives. This bar—perhaps because it was exorbitant in its prices—seldom had more than one self-occupied couple in it at a time. The trouble was too that it really only had one drink—a sweet chocolate liqueur that the waiter improved at a price with cognac—but I got the impression that Martins had no objection to any drink so long as it cast a veil over the present, and the past. On the door was the usual notice saying the bar opened

15

from six till ten, but one just pushed the door and walked through the front rooms. We had a whole small room to ourselves; the only couple were next door, and the waiter, who knew me, left us alone with some caviare sandwiches. It was lucky that we both knew I had an expense account.

Martins said over his second quick drink, 'I'm sorry, but he was the best friend I ever had.'

I couldn't resist saying, knowing what I knew, and because I was anxious to vex him—one learns a lot that way—'That sounds like a cheap novelette.'

He said quickly, 'I write cheap novelettes.'

I had learned something anyway. Until he had had a third drink I was under the impression that he wasn't an easy talker, but I felt fairly certain that he was one of those who turn unpleasant after their fourth glass.

I said, 'Tell me about yourself—and Lime.'

'Look here,' he said, 'I badly need another drink, but I can't keep on scrounging on a stranger. Could you change me a pound or two into Austrian money?'

'Don't bother about that,' I said and called the waiter. 'You can treat me when I come to London on leave. You were going to tell me how you met Lime?'

16

The glass of chocolate liqueur might have been a crystal, the way he looked at it and turned it this way and that. He said, 'It was a long time ago. I don't suppose anyone knows Harry the way I do,' and I thought of the thick file of agents' reports in my office, each claiming the same thing. I believe in my agents; I've sifted them all very thoroughly.

'How long?'

'Twenty years—or a bit more. I met him my first term at school. I can see the place. I can see the notice board and what was on it. I can hear the bell ringing. He was a year older and knew the ropes. He put me wise to a lot of things.' He took a quick dab at his drink and then turned the crystal again as if to see more clearly what there was to see. He said, 'It's funny. I can't remember meeting any woman quite as well.'

'Was he clever at school?'

'Not the way they wanted him to be. But what things he did think up! He was a wonderful planner. I was far better at subjects like History and English than Harry, but I was a hopeless mug when it came to carrying out his plans.' He laughed: he was already beginning, with the help of drink and talk, to throw off the shock of the death. He said, 'I was always the one who got caught.'

17

'That was convenient for Lime.'

'What the hell do you mean?' he asked. Alcoholic irritation was setting in.

'Well, wasn't it?'

'That was my fault, not his. He could have found someone cleverer if he'd chosen, but he liked me.' Certainly, I thought, the child is father to the man, for I too had found Lime patient.

'When did you see him last?'

'Oh, he was over in London six months ago for a medical congress. You know he qualified as a doctor, though he never practised. That was typical of Harry. He just wanted to see if he could do a thing and then he lost interest. But he used to say that it often came in handy.' And that too was true. It was odd how like the Lime he knew was to the Lime I knew: it was only that he looked at Lime's image from a different angle or in a different light. He said, 'One of the things I liked about Harry was his humour.' He gave a grin which took five years off his age. 'I'm a buffoon. I like playing the silly fool, but Harry had real wit. You know, he could have been a first-class light composer if he had worked at it.'

He whistled a tune—it was oddly familiar to me. 'I always remember that. I saw Harry write it. Just in a couple of minutes on the

18

back of an envelope. That was what he always whistled when he had something on his mind. It was his signature tune.' He whistled the tune a second time, and I knew then who had written it—of course it wasn't Harry. I nearly told him so, but what was the point? The tune wavered and went out. He stared down into his glass, drained what was left, and said, 'It's a damned shame to think of him dying the way he did.'

'It was the best thing that ever happened to him,' I said.

He didn't take in my meaning at once: he was a little hazy with the drinks. 'The best thing?'

'Yes.'

'You mean there wasn't any pain?'

'He was lucky in that way, too.'

It was my tone of voice and not my words that caught Martins' attention. He asked gently and dangerously—I could see his right hand tighten—'Are you hinting at something?'

There is no point at all in showing physical courage in all situations: I eased my chair far enough back to be out of reach of his fist. I said, 'I mean that I had his case completed at police headquarters. He would have served a long spell—a very long spell—if it hadn't

19

been for the accident.'

'What for?'

'He was about the worst racketeer who ever made a dirty living in this city.'

I could see him measuring the distance between us and deciding that he couldn't reach me from where he sat. Rollo wanted to hit out, but Martins was steady, careful. Martins, I began to realise, was dangerous. I wondered whether after all I had made a complete mistake: I couldn't see Martins being quite the mug that Rollo had made out. 'You're a policeman?' he asked.

'Yes.'

'I've always hated policemen. They are always either crooked or stupid.'

'Is that the kind of books you write?'

I could see him edging his chair round to block my way out. I caught the waiter's eye and he knew what I meant—there's an advantage in always using the same bar for interviews.

Martins brought out a surface smile and said gently, 'I have to call them sheriffs.'

'Been in America?' It was a silly conversation.

'No. Is this an interrogation?'

'Just interest.'

'Because if Harry was that kind of

racketeer, I must be one too. We always worked together.'

'I daresay he meant to cut you in—somewhere in the organisation. I wouldn't be surprised if he had meant to give you the baby to hold. That was his method at school—you told me, didn't you? And, you see, the headmaster was getting to know a thing or two.'

'You are running true to form, aren't you? I suppose there was some petty racket going on with petrol and you couldn't pin it on anyone, so you've picked a dead man. That's just like a policeman. You're a real policeman, I suppose?'

'Yes, Scotland Yard, but they've put me into a colonel's uniform when I'm on duty.'

He was between me and the door now. I couldn't get away from the table without coming into range. I'm no fighter, and he had six inches of advantage anyway. I said, 'It wasn't petrol.'

'Tyres, saccharin—why don't you policemen catch a few murderers for a change?'

'Well, you could say that murder was part of his racket.'

He pushed the table over with one hand and made a dive at me with the other; the drink confused his calculations. Before he could try again my driver had his arms round him. I said, 'Don't treat him rough. He's only a writer with too much drink in him.'

'Be quiet, can't you, sir,' my driver said. He had an exaggerated sense of officer-class. He would probably have called Lime 'sir'.

'Listen, Callaghan, or whatever your bloody name is . . .'

'Calloway. I'm English, not Irish.'

'I'm going to make you look the biggest bloody fool in Vienna. There's one dead man you aren't going to pin your unsolved crimes on.'

'I see. You're going to find me the real criminal? It sounds like one of your stories.'

'You can let me go, Callaghan. I'd rather make you look the fool you are than black your bloody eye. You'd only have to go to bed for a few days with a black eye. But when I've finished with you, you'll leave Vienna.'

I took out a couple of pounds' worth of bafs and stuck them in his breast pocket. 'These will see you through tonight,' I said, 'and I'll make sure they keep a seat for you on tomorrow's London plane.'

'You can't turn me out. My papers are in order.'

'Yes, but this is like other cities: you need money here. If you change sterling on the black market I'll catch up on you inside twenty-four hours. Let him go.'

Rollo Martins dusted himself down. He said, 'Thanks for the drinks.'

'That's all right.'

'I'm glad I don't have to feel grateful. I suppose they were on expenses?'

'Yes.'

'I'll be seeing you again in a week or two when I've got the dope.' I knew he was angry. I didn't believe then that he was serious. I thought he was putting over an act to cheer up his self-esteem.

'I might come and see you off tomorrow.'

'I shouldn't waste your time. I won't be there.'

'Paine here will show you the way to Sacher's. You can get a bed and dinner there. I'll see to that.'

He stepped to one side as though to make way for the waiter and slashed out at me. I just avoided him, but stumbled against the table. Before he could try again Paine had landed him on the mouth. He went bang over in the alleyway between the tables and came up bleeding from a cut lip. I said, 'I thought you promised not to fight.'

He wiped some of the blood away with his sleeve and said, 'Oh, no, I said I'd rather make you a bloody fool. I didn't say I wouldn't give

23

you a black eye as well.'

I had had a long day and I was tired of Rollo Martins. I said to Paine, 'See him safely into Sacher's. Don't hit him again if he behaves,' and turning away from both of them towards the inner bar (I deserved one more drink), I heard Paine say respectfully to the man he had just knocked down, 'This way, sir. It's only just around the corner.'

# CHAPTER THREE

WHAT happened next I didn't hear from Paine but from Martins a long time afterwards, reconstructing the chain of events that did indeed—though not quite in the way he had expected—prove me to be a fool. Paine simply saw him to the head porter's desk and explained there, 'This gentleman came in on the plane from London. Colonel Calloway says he's to have a room.' Having made that clear, he said, 'Good evening, sir,' and left. He was probably a bit embarrassed by Martins' bleeding lip.

'Had you already got a reservation, sir?' the porter asked.

'No. No, I don't think so,' Martins said in a muffled voice holding his handkerchief to his mouth.

'I thought perhaps you might be Mr. Dexter. We had a room reserved for a week for Mr. Dexter.'

Martins said, 'Oh, I am Mr. Dexter.' He told me later that it occurred to him that Lime might have engaged him a room in that name because perhaps it was Buck Dexter and not Rollo Martins who was to be used for propaganda purposes. A voice said at his elbow, 'I'm so sorry you were not met at the plane, Mr. Dexter. My name's Crabbin.'

The speaker was a stout middle-aged young man with a natural tonsure and one of the thickest pairs of horn-rimmed glasses that Martins had ever seen. He went apologetically on, 'One of our chaps happened to ring up Frankfurt and heard you were on the plane. HQ made one of their usual foolish mistakes and wired you were not coming. Something about Sweden, but the cable was badly mutilated. Directly I heard from Frankfurt I tried to meet the plane, but I just missed you. You got my note?'

Martins held his handkerchief to his mouth and said obscurely, 'Yes. Yes?'

'May I say at once, Mr. Dexter, how excited I am to meet you?'

'Good of you.'

'Ever since I was a boy, I've thought you the greatest novelist of our century.'

Martins winced. It was painful opening his mouth to protest. He took an angry look instead at Mr. Crabbin, but it was impossible to suspect that young man of a practical joke.

'You have a big Austrian public, Mr. Dexter, both for your originals and your translations. Especially for *The Curved*

*Prow*, that's my own favourite.'

Martins was thinking hard. 'Did you say—room for a week?'

'Yes.'

'Very kind of you.'

'Mr. Schmidt here will give you tickets every day, to cover all meals. But I expect you'll need a little pocket money. We'll fix that. Tomorrow we thought you'd like a quiet day—to look about.'

'Yes.'

'Of course any of us are at your service if you need a guide. Then the day after tomorrow in the evening there's a little quiet discussion at the Institute—on the contemporary novel. We thought perhaps you'd say a few words just to set the ball rolling, and then answer questions.'

Martins at that moment was prepared to agree to anything, to get rid of Mr. Crabbin and also to secure a week's free board and lodging; and Rollo, of course, as I was to discover later, had always been prepared to accept any suggestion—for a drink, for a girl, for a joke, for a new excitement. He said now, 'Of course, of course,' into his handkerchief.

'Excuse me, Mr. Dexter, have you got toothache? I know a very good dentist.'

'No. Somebody hit me, that's all.'

27

'Good God! Were they trying to rob you?'

'No, it was a soldier. I was trying to punch his bloody colonel in the eye.' He removed the handkerchief and gave Crabbin a view of his cut mouth. He told me that Crabbin was at a complete loss for words. Martins couldn't understand why because he had never read the work of his great contemporary, Benjamin Dexter: he hadn't even heard of him. I am a great admirer of Dexter, so that I could understand Crabbin's bewilderment. Dexter has been ranked as a stylist with Henry James, but he has a wider feminine streak than his master—indeed his enemies have sometimes described his subtle, complex, wavering style as old-maidish. For a man still just on the right side of fifty his passionate interest in embroidery and his habit of calming a not very tumultuous mind with tatting—a trait beloved by his disciples—certainly to others seems a little affected.

'Have you ever read a book called *The Lone Rider of Santa Fé*?'

'No, I don't think so.'

Martins said, 'This lone rider had his best friend shot by the sheriff of a town called Lost Claim Gulch. The story is how he hunted that sheriff down—quite legally—until his revenge was completed.'

'I never imagined you reading Westerns, Mr. Dexter,' Crabbin said, and it needed all Martins' resolution to stop Rollo saying, 'But I write them.'

'Well, I'm gunning just the same way for Colonel Callaghan.'

'Never heard of him.'

'Heard of Harry Lime?'

'Yes,' Crabbin said cautiously, 'but I didn't really know him.'

'I did. He was my best friend.'

'I shouldn't have thought he was a very—literary character.'

'None of my friends are.'

Crabbin blinked nervously behind the horn-rims. He said with an air of appeasement, 'He was interested in the theatre though. A friend of his—an actress, you know—is learning English at the Institute. He called once or twice to fetch her.'

'Young or old?'

'Oh, young, very young. Not a good actress in my opinion.'

Martins remembered the girl by the grave with her hands over her face. He said, 'I'd like to meet any friend of Harry's.'

'She'll probably be at your lecture.'

'Austrian?'

'She claims to be Austrian, but I suspect

she's Hungarian. She works at the Josefstadt.'

'Why claims to be Austrian?'

'The Russians sometimes get interested in
the Hungarians. I wouldn't be surprised if
Lime had helped her with her papers. She
calls herself Schmidt. Anna Schmidt. You
can't imagine a young English actress calling
herself Smith, can you? And a pretty one, too.
It always struck me as a bit too anonymous to
be true.'

Martins felt he had got all he could from
Crabbin, so he pleaded tiredness, a long day,
promised to ring up in the morning, accepted
ten pounds' worth of bafs for immediate
expenses, and went to his room. It seemed to
him that he was earning money rapidly—twelve pounds in less than an hour.

He *was* tired: he realised that when he
stretched himself out on his bed in his boots.
Within a minute he had left Vienna far behind him and was walking through a dense
wood, ankle-deep in snow. An owl hooted,
and he felt suddenly lonely and scared. He
had an appointment to meet Harry under a
particular tree, but in a wood so dense as this
how could he recognise any one tree from the
rest? Then he saw a figure and ran towards it:
it whistled a familiar tune and his heart lifted

with the relief and joy at not after all being alone. Then the figure turned and it was not Harry at all—just a stranger who grinned at him in a little circle of wet slushy melted snow, while the owl hooted again and again. He woke suddenly to hear the telephone ringing by his bed.

A voice with a trace of foreign accent—only a trace—said, 'Is that Mr. Rollo Martins?'

'Yes.' It was a change to be himself and not Dexter.

'You wouldn't know me,' the voice said unnecessarily, 'but I was a friend of Harry Lime.'

It was a change too to hear anyone claim to be a friend of Harry's. Martins' heart warmed towards the stranger. He said, 'I'd be glad to meet you.'

'I'm just round the corner at the Old Vienna.'

'Wouldn't you make it tomorrow? I've had a pretty awful day with one thing and another.'

'Harry asked me to see that you were all right. I was with him when he died.'

'I thought—' Rollo Martins said and stopped. He had been going to say, 'I thought he died instantaneously,' but something

31

suggested caution. He said instead, 'You haven't told me your name.'

'Kurtz,' the voice said. 'I'd offer to come round to you, only, you know, Austrians aren't allowed in Sacher's.'

'Perhaps we could meet at the Old Vienna in the morning.'

'Certainly,' the voice said, 'if you are *quite* sure that you are all right till then?'

'How do you mean?'

'Harry had it on his mind that you'd be penniless.' Rollo Martins lay back on his bed with the receiver to his ear and thought: Come to Vienna to make money. This was the third stranger to stake him in less than five hours. He said cautiously, 'Oh, I can carry on till I see you.' There seemed no point in turning down a good offer till he knew what the offer was.

'Shall we say eleven, then, at the Old Vienna in the Kärntnerstrasse? I'll be in a brown suit and I'll carry one of your books.'

'That's fine. How did you get hold of one?'

'Harry gave it to me.' The voice had enormous charm and reasonableness, but when Martins had said good night and rung off, he couldn't help wondering how it was that if Harry had been so conscious before he died he had not had a cable sent to stop him. Hadn't

Callaghan too said that Lime had died instantaneously—or without pain, was it?—or had he put the words into Callaghan's mouth? It was then that the idea first lodged firmly in Martins' mind that there was something wrong about Lime's death, something the police had been too stupid to discover. He tried to discover it himself with the help of two cigarettes, but he fell asleep without his dinner and with the mystery still unsolved. It had been a long day, but not quite long enough for that.

# CHAPTER FOUR

'WHAT I disliked about him at first sight,' Martins told me, 'was his toupée. It was one of those obvious toupées—flat and yellow, with the hair cut straight at the back and not fitting close. There *must* be something phoney about a man who won't accept baldness gracefully. He had one of those faces too where the lines have been put in carefully, like a make-up, in the right places—to express charm, whimsicality, lines at the corners of the eyes. He was made up to appeal to romantic schoolgirls.'

This conversation took place some days later—he brought out his whole story when the trail was nearly cold. We were sitting in the Old Vienna at the table he had occupied that first morning with Kurtz, and when he made that remark about the romantic school-girls I saw his rather hunted eyes focus suddenly. It was a girl—just like any other girl, I thought, hurrying by outside in the driving snow.

'Something pretty?'

He brought his gaze back and said, 'I'm off that for ever. You know, Calloway, a time comes in a man's life when he gives up all that sort of thing . . .'

'I see. I thought you were looking at a girl.'

'I was. But only because she reminded me for a moment of Anna—Anna Schmidt.'

'Who's she? Isn't she a girl?'

'Oh, yes, in a way.'

'What do you mean, in a way?'

'She was Harry's girl.'

'Are you taking her over?'

'She's not that kind, Calloway. Didn't you see her at his funeral? I'm not mixing my drinks any more. I've got a hangover to last me a lifetime.'

'You were telling me about Kurtz,' I said.

It appeared that Kurtz was sitting there, making a great show of reading *The Lone Rider of Santa Fé*. When Martins sat down at his table he said with indescribably false enthusiasm, 'It's wonderful how you keep the tension.'

'Tension?'

'Suspense. You're a master at it. At the end of every chapter one's left guessing . . .'

'So you were a friend of Harry's,' Martins said.

'I think, his best,' but Kurtz added with the smallest pause, in which his brain must have registered the error, 'except you of course.'

'Tell me how he died.'

'I was with him. We came out together from the door of his flat and Harry saw a friend he knew across the road—an American called Cooler. He waved to Cooler and started across the road to him when a jeep came tearing round the corner and bowled him over. It was Harry's fault really—not the driver's.'

'Somebody told me he died instantaneously.'

'I wish he had. He died before the ambulance could reach us though.'

'He could speak, then?'

'Yes. Even in his pain he worried about you.'

'What did he say?'

'I can't remember the exact words, Rollo—I may call you Rollo, mayn't I? he always called you that to us. He was anxious that I should look after you when you arrived. See that you were looked after. Get your return ticket for you.' In telling me, Martins said, 'You see I was collecting return tickets as well as cash.'

'But why didn't you cable to stop me?'

'We did, but the cable must have missed you. What with censorship and the zones, cables can take anything up to five days.'

'There was an inquest?'

'Of course.'

'Did you know that the police have a crazy notion that Harry was mixed up in some racket?'

'No. But everyone in Vienna is. We all sell cigarettes and exchange schillings for bafs and that kind of thing. You won't find a single member of the Control Commission who hasn't broken the rules.'

'The police meant something worse than that.'

'They get rather absurd ideas sometimes,' the man with the toupée said cautiously.

'I'm going to stay here till I prove them wrong.'

Kurtz turned his head sharply and the toupée shifted very very slightly. He said, 'What's the good? Nothing can bring Harry back.'

'I'm going to have that police officer run out of Vienna.'

'I don't see what you can do.'

'I'm going to start working back from his death. You were there and this man Cooler and the chauffeur. You can give me their addresses.'

'I don't know the chauffeur's.'

'I can get it from the coroner's records. And then there's Harry's girl . . .'

Kurtz said, 'It will be painful for her.'

'I'm not concerned about her. I'm concerned about Harry.'

'Do you know what it is that the police suspect?'

'No. I lost my temper too soon.'

'Has it occurred to you,' Kurtz said gently, 'that you might dig up something—well, discreditable to Harry?'

'I'll risk that.'

'It will take a bit of time—and money.'

'I've got time and you were going to lend me some money, weren't you?'

'I'm not a rich man,' Kurtz said. 'I promised Harry to see you were all right and that you got your plane back . . .'

'You needn't worry about the money—or the plane,' Martins said. 'But I'll make a bet with you—in pounds sterling—five pounds against two hundred schillings—that there's something queer about Harry's death.'

It was a shot in the dark, but already he had this firm instinctive sense that there was something wrong, though he hadn't yet attached the word 'murder' to the instinct. Kurtz had a cup of coffee half-way to his lips and Martins watched him. The shot apparently went wide; an unaffected hand held the cup to the mouth and Kurtz drank, a little noisily, in long sips. Then he put down the cup and said, 'How do you mean—queer?'

'It was convenient for the police to have a corpse, but wouldn't it have been equally convenient, perhaps, for the real racketeers?' When he had spoken he realised that after all Kurtz had not been unaffected by his wild statement: hadn't he been frozen into caution and calm? The hands of the guilty don't necessarily tremble; only in stories does a dropped glass betray agitation. Tension is more often shown in the studied action. Kurtz had drunk his coffee as though nothing had been said.

'Well—' he took another sip—'of course I wish you luck, though I don't believe there's anything to find. Just ask me for any help you want.'

'I want Cooler's address.'

'Certainly. I'll write it down for you. Here it is. In the American zone.'

'And yours?'

'I've already put it—underneath. I'm unlucky enough to be in the Russian zone—so I shouldn't visit me very late. Things sometimes happen round our way.' He was giving one of his studied Viennese smiles, the charm carefully painted in with a fine brush in the little lines about the mouth and eyes. 'Keep in touch,' he said, 'and if you need any help . . . but I still think you are very unwise.' He picked up *The Lone Rider*. 'I'm so proud to have met you. A master of suspense,' and one hand smoothed the toupée, while another, passing softly over the mouth, brushed out the smile as though it had never been.

# CHAPTER FIVE

MARTINS sat on a hard chair just inside the stage door of the Josefstadt Theatre. He had sent up his card to Anna Schmidt after the matinée, marking it 'a friend of Harry's.' An arcade of little windows, with lace curtains and the lights going out one after another, showed where the artists were packing up for home, for the cup of coffee without sugar, the roll without butter to sustain them for the evening performance. It was like a little street built indoors for a film set, but even indoors it was cold, even cold to a man in a heavy overcoat, so that Martins rose and walked up and down, underneath the little windows. He felt, he said rather like a Romeo who wasn't sure of Juliet's balcony.

He had had time to think: he was calm now, Martins not Rollo was in the ascendant. When a light went out in one of the windows and an actress descended into the passage where he walked, he didn't even turn to take a look. He was done with all that. He thought, Kurtz is right. They are all right. I'm behaving like a romantic fool. I'll just have a word with Anna Schmidt, a word of commiseration, and then I'll pack and go. He had quite forgotten, he told me, the complication of Mr. Crabbin.

A voice over his head called 'Mr. Martins,' and he looked up at the face that watched him from between the curtains a few feet above his head. It wasn't a beautiful face, he firmly explained to me, when I accused him of once again mixing his drinks. Just an honest face; dark hair and eyes which in that light looked brown; a wide forehead, a large mouth which didn't try to charm. No danger anywhere, it seemed to Rollo Martins, of that sudden reckless moment when the scent of hair or a hand against the side alters life. She said, 'Will you come up, please? The second door on the right.'

There are some people, he explained to me carefully, whom one recognises instantaneously as friends. You can be at ease with them because you know that never, never will you be in danger. 'That was Anna,' he said, and I wasn't sure whether the past tense was deliberate or not.

Unlike most actresses' rooms this one was almost bare; no wardrobe packed with clothes, no clutter of cosmetics and grease paints; a dressing-gown on the door, one sweater he recognised from Act II on the only

42

easy chair, a tin of half-used paints and grease. A kettle hummed softly on a gas ring. She said, 'Would you like a cup of tea? Someone sent me a packet last week—sometimes the Americans do, instead of flowers, you know, on the first night.'

'I'd like a cup,' he said, but if there was one thing he hated it was tea. He watched her while she made it, made it, of course, all wrong: the water not on the boil, the teapot unheated, too few leaves. She said, 'I never quite understand why English people like tea.'

He drank his cupful quickly like a medicine and watched her gingerly and delicately sip at hers. He said, 'I wanted very much to see you. About Harry.'

It was the dreadful moment; he could see her mouth stiffen to meet it.

'Yes?'

'I had known him twenty years. I was his friend. We were at school together, you know, and after that—there weren't many months running when we didn't meet . . .'

She said, 'When I got your card, I couldn't say no. But there's nothing really for us to talk about, is there?—nothing.'

'I wanted to hear—'

'He's dead. That's the end. Everything's

43

over, finished. What's the good of talking?'

'We both loved him.'

'I don't know. You can't know a thing like that—afterwards. I don't know anything any more except—'

'Except?'

'That I want to be dead too.'

Martins told me, 'Then I nearly went away. What was the good of tormenting her because of this wild idea of mine? But instead I asked her one question. "Do you know a man called Cooler?"'

'An American?' she asked. 'I think that was the man who brought me some money when Harry died. I didn't want to take it, but he said Harry had been anxious—at the last moment.'

'So he didn't die instantaneously?'

'Oh, no.'

Martins said to me, 'I began to wonder why I had got that idea so firmly into my head, and then I thought it was only the man in the flat who told me so—no one else. I said to her, "He must have been very clear in his head at the end—because he remembered about me too. That seems to show that there wasn't really any pain."'

'That's what I tell myself all the time.'

'Did you see the doctor?'

44

'Once. Harry sent me to him. He was Harry's own doctor. He lived near-by, you see.'

Martins suddenly saw in that odd chamber of the mind that constructs such pictures, instantaneously, irrationally, a desert place, a body on the ground, a group of birds gathered. Perhaps it was a scene from one of his own books, not yet written, forming at the gate of consciousness. Immediately it faded, he thought how odd that they were all there, just at that moment, all Harry's friends— Kurtz, the doctor, this man Cooler; only the two people who loved him seemed to have been missing. He said, 'And the driver? Did you hear his evidence?'

'He was upset, scared. But Cooler's evidence exonerated him, and Kurtz'. No, it wasn't his fault, poor man. I've often heard Harry say what a careful driver he was.'

'He knew Harry too?' Another bird flapped down and joined the others round the silent figure on the sand who lay face down. Now he could tell that it was Harry, by the clothes, by the attitude like that of a boy asleep in the grass at a playing field's edge, on a hot summer afternoon.

Somebody called outside the window, 'Fräulein Schmidt.'

She said, 'They don't like one to stay too long. It uses up *their* electricity.'

He had given up the idea of sparing her anything. He told her, 'The police say they were going to arrest Harry. They'd pinned some racket on him.'

She took the news in much the same way as Kurtz. 'Everybody's in a racket.'

'I don't believe he was in anything serious.'

'No.'

'But he may have been framed. Do you know a man named Kurtz?'

'I don't think so.'

'He wears a toupée.'

'Oh.' He could tell that that struck home. He said, 'Don't you think that it was odd they were all there—at the death? Everybody knew Harry. Even the driver, the doctor . . .'

She said with hopeless calm, 'I've wondered that too, though I didn't know about Kurtz. I wondered whether they'd murdered him, but what's the use of wondering?'

'I'm going to get those bastards,' Rollo Martins said.

'It won't do any good. Perhaps the police are right. Perhaps poor Harry got mixed up—'

'Fräulein Schmidt,' the voice called again.

'I must go.'

'I'll walk with you a bit of the way.'

The dark was almost down; the snow had ceased for a while to fall, and the great statues of the Ring, the prancing horses, the chariots and eagles, were gun-shot grey with the end of evening light. 'It's better to give up and forget,' Anna said. The moony snow lay ankle-deep on the unswept pavements.

'Will you give me the doctor's address?'

They stood in the shelter of a wall while she wrote it down for him.

'And yours too?'

'Why do you want that?'

'I might have news for you.'

'There isn't any news that would do any good now.' He watched her from a distance board her tram, bowing her head against the wind, a dark question mark on the snow.

# CHAPTER SIX

AN amateur detective has this advantage over the professional, that he doesn't work set hours. Rollo Martins was not confined to the eight-hour day: his investigations didn't have to pause for meals. In his one day he covered as much ground as one of my men would have covered in two, and he had this initial advantage over us, that he was Harry's friend. He was, as it were, working from inside, while we pecked at the perimeter.

Dr. Winkler was at home. Perhaps he would not have been at home to a police officer. Again Martins had marked his card with the same phrase: 'A friend of Harry Lime's.'

Dr. Winkler's waiting-room reminded Martins of an antique shop—an antique shop that specialises in religious objets d'art. There were more crucifixes than he could count, none of later date probably than the seventeenth century. There were statues in wood and ivory. There were a number of reliquaries: little bits of bone marked with saints' names and set in oval frames on a background of tinfoil. If they were genuine, what an odd fate it was, Martins thought, for a portion of Saint Susanna's knuckle to come to rest in Dr. Winkler's waiting room. Even the high-backed hideous chairs looked as if they had once been sat in by cardinals. The room was stuffy, and one expected the smell of incense. In a small gold casket was a splinter of the True Cross. A sneeze disturbed him.

Dr. Winkler was the cleanest doctor Martins had ever seen. He was very small and neat, in a black tail-coat and a high stiff collar; his little black moustache was like an evening tie. He sneezed again: perhaps he was cold because he was so clean. He said, 'Mr. Martins?'

An irresistible desire to sully Dr. Winkler assailed Rollo Martins. He said, 'Dr. Winkle?'

'Dr. Winkler.'

'You've got an interesting collection here.'

'Yes.'

'These saints' bones . . .'

'The bones of chickens and rabbits.' Dr. Winkler took a large white handkerchief out of his sleeve rather as though he were a conjurer producing his country's flag, and blew his nose neatly and thoroughly twice, closing each nostril in turn. You expected him to throw away the handkerchief after one use. 'Would you mind, Mr. Martins, telling me the

49

purpose of your visit? I have a patient waiting.'

'We were both friends of Harry Lime.'

'I was his medical adviser,' Dr. Winkler
corrected him and waited obstinately between
the crucifixes.

'I arrived too late for the inquest. Harry
had invited me out here to help him in something. I don't quite know what. I didn't hear
of his death till I arrived.'

'Very sad,' Dr. Winkler said.

'Naturally, under the circumstances, I
want to hear all I can.'

'There is nothing I can tell you that you
don't know. He was knocked over by a car. He
was dead when I arrived.'

'Would he have been conscious at all?'

'I understand he was for a short time, while
they carried him into the house.'

'In great pain?'

'Not necessarily.'

'You are quite certain that it was an accident?'

Dr. Winkler put out a hand and
straightened a crucifix. 'I was not there. My
opinion is limited to the cause of death. Have
you any reason to be dissatisfied?'

The amateur has another advantage over
the professional: he can be reckless. He can

tell unnecessary truths and propound wild theories. Martins said, 'The police have implicated Harry in a very serious racket. It seemed to me that he might have been murdered—or even killed himself.'

'I am not competent to pass an opinion,' Dr. Winkler said.

'Do you know a man called Cooler?'

'I don't think so.'

'He was there when Harry was killed.'

'Then of course I have met him. He wears a toupée.'

'That was Kurtz.'

Dr. Winkler was not only the cleanest, he was also the most cautious doctor that Martins had ever met. His statements were so limited that you could not for a moment doubt their veracity. He said, 'There was a second man there.' If he had to diagnose a case of scarlet fever he would, you felt, have confined himself to a statement that a rash was visible, that the temperature was so and so. He would never find himself in error at an inquest.

'Had you been Harry's doctor for long?' He seemed an odd man for Harry to choose— Harry who liked men with a certain recklessness, men capable of making mistakes.

'For about a year.'

51

'Well, it's good of you to have seen me.' Dr. Winkler bowed. When he bowed there was a very slight creak as though his shirt were made of celluloid. 'I mustn't keep you from your patients any longer.' Turning away from Dr. Winkler, he confronted yet another crucifix, the figure hanging with arms above the head: a face of elongated El Greco agony. 'That's a strange crucifix,' he said.

'Jansenist,' Dr. Winkler commented and closed his mouth sharply as though he had been guilty of giving away too much information.

'Never heard the word. Why are the arms above the head?'

Dr. Winkler said reluctantly, 'Because He died, in their view, only for the elect.'

# CHAPTER SEVEN

As I see it, turning over my files, the notes of conversations, the statements of various characters, it would have been still possible, at this moment, for Rollo Martins to have left Vienna safely. He had shown an unhealthy curiosity, but the disease had been checked at every point. Nobody had given anything away. The smooth wall of deception had as yet shown no real crack to his roaming fingers. When Rollo Martins left Dr. Winkler's he was in no danger. He could have gone home to bed at Sacher's and slept with a quiet mind. He could even have visited Cooler at this stage without trouble. No one was seriously disturbed. Unfortunately for him—and there would always be periods of his life when he bitterly regretted it—he chose to go back to Harry's flat. He wanted to talk to the little vexed man who said he had seen the accident —or had he really not said so much? There was a moment in the dark frozen street when he was inclined to go straight to Cooler, to complete his picture of those sinister birds who sat around Harry's body, but Rollo, being Rollo, decided to toss a coin and the coin fell for the other action, and the deaths of two men.

Perhaps the little man—who bore the name of Koch—had drunk a glass too much of wine, perhaps he had simply spent a good day at the office, but this time, when Rollo Martins rang his bell, he was friendly and quite ready to talk. He had just finished dinner and had crumbs on his moustache. 'Ah, I remember you. You are Herr Lime's friend.'

He welcomed Martins in with great cordiality and introduced him to a mountainous wife whom he obviously kept under very strict control. 'Ah, in the old days I would have offered you a cup of coffee, but now—'

Martins passed round his cigarette case and the atmosphere of cordiality deepened. 'When you rang yesterday I was a little abrupt,' Herr Koch said, 'but I had a touch of migraine and my wife was out, so I had to answer the door myself.'

'Did you tell me that you had actually seen the accident?'

Herr Koch exchanged glances with his wife. 'The inquest is over, Ilse. There is no harm. You can trust my judgment. The gentleman is a friend. Yes, I saw the accident, but you are the only one who knows. When I say

54

that I saw it, perhaps I should say that I heard it. I heard the brakes put on and the sound of the skid, and I got to the window in time to see them carry the body to the house.'

'But didn't you give evidence?'

'It is better not to be mixed up in such things. My office cannot spare me. We are short of staff, and of course I did not actually *see*—'

'But you told me yesterday how it happened.'

'That was how they described it in the papers.'

'Was he in great pain?'

'He was dead. I looked right down from my window here and I saw his face. I know when a man is dead. You see, it is, in a way, my business. I am the head clerk at the mortuary.'

'But the others say that he did not die at once.'

'Perhaps they don't know death as well as I do.'

'He was dead, of course, when the doctor arrived. He told me that.'

'He was dead at once. You can take the word of a man who knows.'

'I think, Herr Koch, that you should have given evidence.'

'One must look after oneself, Herr Martins.

I was not the only one who should have been there.'

'How do you mean?'

'There were three people who helped to carry your friend to the house.'

'I know—two men and the driver.'

'The driver stayed where he was. He was very much shaken, poor man.'

'Three men . . .' It was as though suddenly, fingering that bare wall, his fingers had encountered, not so much a crack perhaps, but at least a roughness that had not been smoothed away by the careful builders.

'Can you describe the men?'

But Herr Koch was not trained to observe the living: the only man with the toupée had attracted his eyes—the other two were just men, neither tall nor short, thick nor thin. He had seen them from far above, foreshortened, bent over their burden; they had not looked up, and he had quickly looked away and closed the window, realising at once the wisdom of not being seen himself.

'There was no evidence I could really give, Herr Martins.'

No evidence, Martins thought, no evidence! He no longer doubted that murder had been done. Why else had they lied about the moment of death? They wanted to quieten with their gifts of money and their plane ticket the only two friends Harry had in Vienna. And the third man? Who was he?

He said, 'Did you see Herr Lime go out?'

'No.'

'Did you hear a scream?'

'Only the brakes, Herr Martins.'

It occurred to Martins that there was nothing—except the word of Kurtz and Cooler and the driver—to prove that in fact Harry had been killed at that precise moment. There was the medical evidence, but that could not prove more than that he had died, say, within a half-hour, and in any case the medical evidence was only as strong as Dr. Winkler's word: that clean, controlled man creaking among his crucifixes.

'Herr Martins, it just occurs to me—you are staying in Vienna?'

'Yes.'

'If you need accommodation and spoke to the authorities quickly, you might secure Herr Lime's flat. It is a requisitioned property.'

'Who has the keys?'

'I have them.'

'Could I see the flat?'

'Ilse, the keys.'

Herr Koch led the way into the flat that

had been Harry's. In the little dark hall there was still the smell of cigarette smoke—the Turkish cigarettes that Harry always smoked. It seemed odd that a man's smell should cling in the folds of curtains so long after the man himself had become dead matter, a gas, a decay. One light, in a heavily beaded shade, left them in semi-darkness, fumbling for door handles.

The living-room was completely bare—it seemed to Martins too bare. The chairs had been pushed up against the walls; the desk at which Harry must have written was free from dust or any papers. The parquet reflected the light like a mirror. Herr Koch opened a door and showed the bedroom: the bed neatly made with clean sheets. In the bathroom not even a used razor blade indicated that a few days ago a living man had occupied it. Only the dark hall and the cigarette smell gave a sense of occupation.

'You see,' Herr Koch said, 'it is quite ready for a newcomer. Ilse has cleaned up.'

That she certainly had done. After a death there should have been more litter left than this. A man can't go suddenly and unexpectedly on his longest journey without forgetting this or that, without leaving a bill unpaid, an official form unanswered, the photograph of a girl. 'Were there no papers, Herr Koch?'

'Herr Lime was always a very tidy man. His waste-paper basket was full and his brief-case, but his friend fetched that away.'

'His friend?'

'The gentleman with the toupée.'

It was possible, of course, that Lime had not taken the journey so unexpectedly, and it occurred to Martins that Lime had perhaps hoped he would arrive in time to help. He said to Herr Koch, 'I believe my friend was mur-dered.'

'Murdered?' Herr Koch's cordiality was snuffed out by the word. He said, 'I would not have asked you in here if I had thought you would talk such nonsense.'

'Why should it be nonsense?'

'We do not have murders in this zone.'

'All the same your evidence may be very valuable.'

'I have no evidence. I saw nothing. I am not concerned. You must leave here at once please. You have been very inconsiderate.' He hustled Martins back through the hall; already the smell of the smoke was fading a little more. Herr Koch's last word before he slammed his own door was, 'It's no concern of mine.' Poor Herr Koch! We do not choose our concerns. Later, when I was questioning Martins closely, I said to him, 'Did you see anybody at all on the stairs, or in the street outside?'

'Nobody.' He had everything to gain by remembering some chance passer-by, and I believed him. He said, 'I noticed myself how quiet and dead the whole street looked. Part of it had been bombed, you know, and the moon was shining on the snow slopes. It was so very silent. I could hear my own feet creaking in the snow.'

'Of course it proves nothing. There is a basement where anybody who had followed you could have hidden.'

'Yes.'

'Or your whole story may be phoney.'

'Yes.'

'The trouble is I can see no motive for you to have done it. It's true you are already guilty of getting money on false pretences. You came out here to join Lime, perhaps to help him . . .'

Martins said to me, 'What was this precious racket you keep on hinting at?'

'I'd have told you all the facts when I first saw you if you hadn't lost your temper so damned quickly. Now I don't think I shall be acting wisely to tell you. It would be disclosing official information, and your contacts, you know, don't inspire confidence. A girl with phoney papers supplied by Lime, this man Kurtz . . .'

'Dr. Winkler . . .'

'I've got nothing against Dr. Winkler. No, if you are phoney, you don't need the information, but it might help you to learn exactly what we know. You see, our facts are not complete.'

'I bet they aren't. I could invent a better detective than you in my bath.'

'Your literary style does not do your namesake justice.' Whenever he was reminded of Mr. Crabbin, that poor harassed representative of the British Cultural Relations Society, Rollo Martins turned pink, with annoyance, embarrassment, shame. That too inclined me to trust him.

He had certainly given Crabbin some uncomfortable hours. On returning to Sacher's Hotel after his interview with Herr Koch he had found a desperate note waiting for him from the representative.

'I have been trying to locate you all day,' Crabbin wrote. 'It is essential that we should get together and work out a proper programme for you. This morning by telephone I have arranged lectures at Innsbruck and

61

Salzburg for next week, but I must have your consent to the subjects, so that proper programmes can be printed. I would suggest two lectures: "The Crisis of Faith in the Western World" (you are very respected here as a Christian writer, but this lecture should be quite unpolitical and no references should be made to Russia or communism) and "The Technique of the Contemporary Novel". The same lectures would be given in Vienna. Apart from this, there are a great many people here who would like to meet you, and I want to arrange a cocktail party for early next week. But for all this I must have a few words with you.' The letter ended on a note of acute anxiety. 'You will be at the discussion tomorrow night, won't you? We all expect you at 8.30 and, needless to say, look forward to your coming. I will send transport to the hotel at 8.15 sharp.'

Rollo Martins read the letter and, without bothering any further about Mr. Crabbin, went to bed.

# CHAPTER EIGHT

AFTER two drinks Rollo Martins' mind would always turn towards women—in a vague, sentimental, romantic way, as a Sex, in general. After three drinks, like a pilot who dives to find direction, he would begin to focus on one available girl. If he had not been offered a third drink by Cooler, he would probably not have gone quite so soon to Anna Schmidt's house, and if—but there are too many 'ifs' in my style of writing, for it is my profession to balance possibilities, human possibilities, and the drive of destiny can never find a place in my files.

Martins had spent his lunch-time reading up the reports of the inquest, thus again demonstrating the superiority of the amateur to the professional, and making him more vulnerable to Cooler's liquor (which the professional in duty bound would have refused). It was nearly five o'clock when he reached Cooler's flat, which was over an ice-cream parlour in the American zone: the bar below was full of G.I.s with their girls, and the clatter of the long spoons and the curious free unformed laughter followed him up the stairs.

63

The Englishman who objects to Americans in general usually carries in his mind's eye just such an exception as Cooler: a man with tousled grey hair and a worried kindly face and long-sighted eyes, the kind of humanitarian who turns up in a typhus epidemic or a world war or a Chinese famine long before his countrymen have discovered the place in an atlas. Again the card marked 'Harry's friend' was like an entrance ticket. Cooler was in officer's uniform, with mysterious letters on his flash, and no badges of rank, although his maid referred to him as Colonel Cooler. His warm frank handclasp was the most friendly act that Martins had encountered in Vienna.

'Any friend of Harry is all right with me,' Cooler said. 'I've heard of you, of course.'

'From Harry?'

'I'm a great reader of Westerns,' Cooler said, and Martins believed him as he did not believe Kurtz.

'I wondered—you were there, weren't you?—if you'd tell me about Harry's death.'

'It was a terrible thing,' Cooler said. 'I was just crossing the road to go to Harry. He and Mr. Kurtz were on the sidewalk. Maybe if I hadn't started across the road, he'd have stayed where he was. But he saw me and stepped straight off to meet me and this jeep—it was terrible, terrible. The driver braked, but he didn't stand a chance. Have a Scotch, Mr. Martins. It's silly of me, but I get shaken up when I think of it.' He said as he splashed in the soda, 'In spite of this uniform, I'd never seen a man killed before.'

'Was the other man in the car?'

Cooler took a long pull and then measured what was left with his tired kindly eyes. 'What man would you be referring to, Mr. Martins?'

'I was told there was another man there.'

'I don't know how you got that idea. You'll find all about it in the inquest reports.' He poured out two more generous drinks. 'There were just the three of us—me and Mr. Kurtz and the driver. The doctor, of course. I expect you were thinking of the doctor.'

'This man I was talking to happened to look out of a window—he has the next flat to Harry's—and he said he saw three men and the driver. That's before the doctor arrived.'

'He didn't say that in court.'

'He didn't want to get involved.'

'You'll never teach these Europeans to be good citizens. It was his duty.' Cooler brooded sadly over his glass. 'It's an odd thing, Mr. Martins, with accidents. You'll never get two reports that coincide. Why, even Mr. Kurtz and I disagreed about details.

The thing happens so suddenly, you aren't concerned to notice things, until bang crash, and then you have to reconstruct, remember. I expect he got too tangled up trying to sort out what happened before and what after, to distinguish the four of us.'

'The four?'

'I was counting Harry. What else did he see, Mr. Martins.'

'Nothing of interest—except he says Harry was dead when he was carried to the house.'

'Well, he was dying—not much difference there. Have another drink, Mr. Martins?'

'No, I don't think I will.'

'Well, I'd like another spot. I was very fond of your friend, Mr. Martins, and I don't like talking about it.'

'Perhaps one more—to keep you company. Do you know Anna Schmidt?' Martins asked, while the whisky tingled on his tongue.

'Harry's girl? I met her once, that's all. As a matter of fact, I helped Harry fix her papers. Not the sort of thing I should confess to a stranger, I suppose, but you have to break the rules sometimes. Humanity's a duty too.'

'What was wrong?'

'She was Hungarian and her father had been a Nazi, so they said. She was scared the Russians would pick her up.'

'Why should they want to?'

'We can't always figure out why they do these things. Perhaps just to show that it's not healthy being friends with an Englishman.'

'But she lives in the British zone.'

'That wouldn't stop them. It's only five minutes ride in a jeep from the Commandatura. The streets aren't well lighted, and you haven't many police around.'

'You took her some money from Harry, didn't you?'

'Yes, but I wouldn't have mentioned that. Did she tell you?'

The telephone rang, and Cooler drained his glass. 'Hullo,' he said. 'Why, yes. This is Colonel Cooler.' Then he sat with the receiver at his ear and an expression of sad patience, while some voice a long way off drained into the room. 'Yes,' he said once. 'Yes.' His eyes dwelt on Martins' face, but they seemed to be looking a long way beyond him: flat and tired and kind, they might have been gazing out across the sea. He said, 'You did quite right,' in a tone of commendation, and then, with a touch of asperity, 'Of course they will be delivered. I gave my word. Goodbye.'

He put the receiver down and passed a hand across his forehead wearily. It was as though he were trying to remember something he had to do. Martins said, 'Had you heard anything of this racket the police talk about?'

'I'm sorry. What's that?'

'They say Harry was mixed up in some racket.'

'Oh, no,' Cooler said. 'No. That's quite impossible. He had a great sense of duty.'

'Kurtz seemed to think it was possible.'

'Kurtz doesn't understand how an Anglo-Saxon feels,' Cooler replied.

# CHAPTER NINE

IT was nearly dark when Martins made his way along the banks of the canal: across the water lay the half-destroyed Diana baths and in the distance the great black circle of the Prater Wheel, stationary above the ruined houses. Over there across the grey water was the second Bezirk, in Russian ownership. St. Stefanskirche shot its enormous wounded spire into the sky above the Inner City, and, coming up the Kärntnerstrasse, Martins passed the lit door of the Military Police station. The four men of the International Patrol were climbing into their jeep; the Russian M.P. sat beside the driver (for the Russians had that day taken over the chair for the next four weeks) and the Englishman, the Frenchman, and the American mounted behind. The third stiff whisky fumed into Martins' brain, and he remembered the girl in Amsterdam, the girl in Paris; loneliness moved along the crowded pavement at his side. He passed the corner of the street where Sacher's lay and went on. Rollo was in control and moved towards the only girl he knew in Vienna.

I asked him how he knew where she lived.

69

Oh, he said, he'd looked up the address she had given him the night before, in bed, studying a map. He wanted to know his way about, and he was good with maps. He could memorise turnings and street names easily because he always went one way on foot.

'One way?'

'I mean when I'm calling on a girl—or someone.'

He hadn't, of course, known that she would be in, that her play was not on that night in the Josefstadt, or perhaps he had memorised that too from the posters. In at any rate she was, if you could really call it being in, sitting alone in an unheated room, with the bed disguised as a divan, and a typewritten script lying open at the first page on the inadequate too-fancy topply table—because her thoughts were so far from being 'in'. He said awkwardly (and nobody could have said, not even Rollo, how much his awkwardness was part of his technique), 'I thought I'd just look in and look you up. You see, I was passing . . .'

'Passing? Where to?' It had been a good half an hour's walk from the Inner City to the rim of the English zone, but he always had a reply. 'I had too much whisky with Colonel Cooler. I needed a walk and I just happened to find myself this way.'

'I can't give you a drink here. Except tea. There's some of that packet left.'

'No, no thank you.' He said, 'You are busy,' looking at the script.

'I didn't get beyond the first line.'

He picked it up and read: '*Enter Louise.* LOUISE: I heard a child crying.'

'Can I stay a little?' he asked with a gentleness that was more Martins than Rollo.

'I wish you would.' He slumped down on the divan, and he told me a long time later (for lovers talk and reconstruct the smallest details if they can find a listener) that there it was he took his second real look at her. She stood there as awkward as himself in a pair of old flannel trousers which had been patched badly in the seat; she stood with her legs firmly straddled as though she were opposing someone and was determined to hold her ground—a small rather stocky figure with any grace she had folded and put away for use professionally.

'One of those bad days?' he asked.

'It's always bad about this time.' She explained, 'He used to look in, and when I heard you ring, just for a moment, I thought . . .' She sat down on a hard chair opposite him and said, 'Please talk. You knew him. Just tell me anything.'

And so he talked. The sky blackened outside the window while he talked. He noticed
after a while that their hands had met. He
said to me, 'I never meant to fall in love, not
with Harry's girl.'

'When did it happen?' I asked him.

'It was very cold and I got up to close the
window curtains. I only noticed my hand was
on hers when I took it away. As I stood up I
looked down at her face and she was looking
up. It wasn't a beautiful face—that was the
trouble. It was a face to live with, day in, day
out. A face for wear. I felt as though I'd come
into a new country where I couldn't speak the
language. I had always thought it was beauty
one loved in a woman. I stood there at the curtains, waiting to pull them, looking out. I
couldn't see anything but my own face, looking back into the room, looking for her. She
said, "And what did Harry do that time?" and
I wanted to say, "Damn Harry. He's dead.
We both loved him, but he's dead. The dead
are made to be forgotten." Instead, of course,
all I said was, "What do you think? He just
whistled his old tune as if nothing was the
matter," and I whistled it to her as well as I
could. I heard her catch her breath, and I
looked round and before I could think: Is this
the right way, the right card, the right

gambit?—I'd already said, "He's dead. You can't go on remembering him for ever."'

She said, 'I know, but perhaps something will happen first.'

'What do you mean—something happen?'

'Oh, I mean, perhaps there'll be another war, or I'll die, or the Russians will take me.'

'You'll forget him in time. You'll fall in love again.'

'I know, but I don't want to. Don't you see I don't want to?'

So Rollo Martins came back from the window and sat down on the divan again. When he had risen half a minute before he had been the friend of Harry, comforting Harry's girl; now he was a man in love with Anna Schmidt who had been in love with a man they had both once known called Harry Lime. He didn't speak again that evening about the past. Instead he began to tell her of the people he had seen. 'I can believe anything of Winkler,' he told her, 'but Cooler—I liked Cooler. He was the only one of his friends who stood up for Harry. The trouble is, if Cooler's right, then Koch is wrong, and I really thought I had something there.'

'Who's Koch?'

He explained how he had returned to Harry's flat and he described his interview

73

with Koch, the story of the third man.

'If it's true,' she said, 'it's very important.'

'It doesn't prove anything. After all, Koch backed out of the inquest; so might this stranger.'

'That's not the point,' she said. 'It means that *they* lied: Kurtz and Cooler.'

'They might have lied so as not to inconvenience this fellow—if he was a friend.'

'Yet another friend—on the spot. And where's your Cooler's honesty then?'

'What do we do? Koch clamped down like an oyster and turned me out of his flat.'

'He won't turn me out,' she said, 'or his Ilse won't.'

They walked up the long road to the flat together; the snow clogged on their shoes and made them move slowly like convicts weighed down by irons. Anna Schmidt said, 'Is it far?'

'Not very far now. Do you see that knot of people up the road? It's somewhere about there.' The group was like a splash of ink on the whiteness, a splash that flowed, changed shape, spread out. When they came a little nearer Martins said, 'I think that's his block. What do you suppose this is, a political demonstration?'

Anna Schmidt stopped. She said, 'Who else have you told about Koch?'

'Only you and Colonel Cooler. Why?'

'I'm frightened. It reminds me . . .' She had her eyes fixed on the crowd and he never knew what memory out of her confused past had risen to warn her. 'Let's go away,' she implored him.

'You're crazy. We're on to something here, something big . . .'

'I'll wait for you.'

'But you're going to talk to him.'

'Find out first what all those people . . .' She said strangely for one who worked behind the footlights, 'I hate crowds.'

He walked slowly on alone, the snow caking on his heels. It wasn't a political meeting, for no one was making a speech. He had the impression of heads turning to watch him come, as though he were somebody who was expected. When he reached the fringe of the little crowd, he knew for certain that it was the house. A man looked hard at him and said, 'Are you another of them?'

'What do you mean?'

'The police.'

'No. What are they doing?'

'They've been in and out all day.'

'What's everybody waiting for?'

'They want to see him brought out.'

'Who?'

75

'Herr Koch.' It occurred vaguely to Martins that somebody besides himself had discovered Herr Koch's failure to give evidence, though that was hardly a police matter. He said, 'What's he done?'

'Nobody knows that yet. They can't make their minds up in there—it might be suicide, you see, and it might be murder.'

'Herr Koch?'

'Of course.'

A small child came up to his informant and pulled at his hand. 'Papa, Papa.' He wore a wool cap on his head, like a gnome; his face was pinched and blue with cold.

'Yes, my dear, what is it?'

'I heard them talking through the grating, Papa.'

'Oh, you cunning little one. Tell us what you heard, Hansel.'

'I heard Frau Koch crying, Papa.'

'Was that all, Hansel?'

'No. I heard the big man talking, Papa.'

'Ah, you cunning little Hansel. Tell Papa what he said.'

'He said, "Can you tell me, Frau Koch, what the foreigner looked like?"'

'Ha, ha, you see, they think it's murder. And who's to say they are wrong? Why should Herr Koch cut his own throat in the basement?'

'Papa, Papa.'

'Yes, little Hansel?'

'When I looked through the grating, I could see some blood on the coke.'

'What a child you are. How could you tell it was blood? The snow leaks everywhere.' The man turned to Martins and said, 'The child has such an imagination. Maybe he will be a writer when he grows up.'

The pinched face stared solemnly up at Martins. The child said, 'Papa.'

'Yes, Hansel?'

'He's a foreigner too.'

The man gave a big laugh that caused a dozen heads to turn. 'Listen to him, sir, listen,' he said proudly. 'He thinks you did it just because you are a foreigner. As though there weren't more foreigners here these days than Viennese.'

'Papa, Papa.'

'Yes, Hansel?'

'They are coming out.'

A knot of police surrounded the covered stretcher which they lowered carefully down the steps for fear of sliding on the trodden snow. The man said, 'They can't get an ambulance into this street because of the ruins. They have to carry it round the corner.'

Frau Koch came out at the tail of the procession; she had a shawl over her head and an old sackcloth coat. Her thick shape looked like a snowman as she sank in a drift at the pavement's edge. Someone gave her a hand and she looked round with a lost hopeless gaze at this crowd of strangers. If there were friends there she did not recognise them, looking from face to face. Martins bent as she passed, fumbling at his shoelace, but looking up from the ground he saw at his own eyes' level the scrutinising cold-blooded gnome-gaze of little Hansel.

Walking back down the street towards Anna, he looked back once. The child was pulling at his father's hand and he could see the lips forming round those syllables like the refrain of a grim ballad, 'Papa, Papa.'

He said to Anna, 'Koch has been murdered. Come away from here.' He walked as rapidly as the snow would let him, turning this corner and that. The child's suspicion and alertness seemed to spread like a cloud over the city— they could not walk fast enough to evade its shadow. He paid no attention when Anna said to him, 'Then what Koch said was true. There *was* a third man,' nor a little later when she said, 'It must have been murder. You don't kill a man to hide anything less.'

The tramcars flashed like icicles at the end of the street: they were back at the Ring. Martins said, 'You had better go home alone. I'll keep away from you awhile till things have sorted out.'

'But nobody can suspect you.'

'They are asking about the foreigner who called on Koch yesterday. There may be some unpleasantness for a while.'

'Why don't you go to the police?'

'They are so stupid. I don't trust them. See what they've pinned on Harry. And then I tried to hit this man Callaghan. They'll have it in for me. The least they'll do is send me away from Vienna. But if I stay quiet—there's only one person who can give me away. Cooler.'

'And he won't want to.'

'Not if he's guilty. But then I can't believe he's guilty.'

Before she left him, she said, 'Be careful. Koch knew so very little and they murdered him. You know as much as Koch.'

The warning stayed in his brain all the way to Sacher's: after nine o'clock the streets are very empty, and he would turn his head at every padding step coming up the street behind him, as though that third man whom they had protected so ruthlessly

79

were following him like an executioner. The Russian sentry outside the Grand Hotel looked rigid with the cold, but he was human, he had a face, an honest peasant face with Mongol eyes. The third man had no face: only the top of a head seen from a window. At Sacher's Mr. Schmidt said, 'Colonel Calloway has been in, asking for you, sir. I think you'll find him in the bar.'

'Back in a moment,' Martins said and walked straight out of the hotel again: he wanted time to think. But immediately he stepped outside a man came forward, touched his cap, and said firmly, 'Please, sir.' He flung open the door of a khaki-painted truck with a Union Jack on the windscreen and firmly urged Martins within. He surrendered without protest; sooner or later, he felt sure, inquiries would be made; he had only pretended optimism to Anna Schmidt.

The driver drove too fast for safety on the frozen road, and Martins protested. All he got in reply was a sullen grunt and a muttered sentence containing the word 'orders'. 'Have you orders to kill me?' Martins said and got no reply at all. He caught sight of the Titans on the Hofburg balancing great globes of snow above their heads, and then they plunged into ill-lit streets beyond, where he lost all sense of direction.

'Is it far?' But the driver paid no attention at all. At least, Martins thought, I am not under arrest: they have not sent a guard; I am being invited—wasn't that the word they used?—to visit the station to make a statement.

The car drew up and the driver led the way up two flights of stairs; he rang the bell of a great double door, and Martins was aware of many voices beyond it. He turned sharply to the driver and said, 'Where the hell . . .?' but the driver was already half-way down the stairs, and already the door was opening. His eyes were dazzled from the darkness by the lights inside; he heard but he could hardly see the advance of Crabbin. 'Oh, Mr. Dexter, we have been so anxious, but better late than never. Let me introduce you to Miss Wilbraham and the Gräfin von Meyersdorf.'

A buffet laden with coffee cups; an urn steamed; a woman's face shiny with exertion; two young men with the happy intelligent faces of sixth-formers; and, huddled in the background, like faces in a family album, a multitude of the old-fashioned, the dingy, the earnest and cheery features of constant readers. Martins looked behind him, but the door had closed.

81

He said desperately to Mr. Crabbin, 'I'm sorry, but—'

'Don't think any more about it,' Mr. Crabbin said. 'One cup of coffee and then let's go on to the discussion. We have a very good gathering tonight. They'll put you on your mettle, Mr. Dexter.' One of the young men placed a cup in his hand, the other shovelled in sugar before he could say he preferred his coffee unsweetened. The youngest man breathed into his ear, 'Afterwards would you mind signing one of your books, Mr. Dexter?' A large woman in black silk bore down upon him and said, 'I don't mind if the Gräfin does hear me, Mr. Dexter, but I don't like your books, I don't approve of them. I think a novel should tell a good story.'

'So do I,' Martins said hopelessly.

'Now, Mrs. Bannock, wait for question time.'

'I know I'm downright, but I'm sure Mr. Dexter values *honest* criticism.'

An old lady, whom he supposed was the Gräfin, said, 'I do not read many English books, Mr. Dexter, but I am told that yours . . .'

'Do you mind drinking up?' Crabbin said and hustled him through into an inner room where a number of elderly people were sitting on a semi-circle of chairs with an air of sad patience.

Martins was not able to tell me very much about the meeting; his mind was still dazed with the death; when he looked up he expected to see at any moment the child Hansel and hear that persistent informative refrain. 'Papa, Papa.' Apparently Crabbin opened the proceedings, and, knowing Crabbin, I am sure that it was a very lucid, very fair and unbiased picture of the contemporary English novel. I have heard him give that talk so often, varied only by the emphasis given to the work of the particular English visitor. He would have touched lightly on various problems of technique—the point of view, the passage of time—and then he would have declared the meeting open for questions and discussions.

Martins missed the first question altogether, but luckily Crabbin filled the gap and answered it satisfactorily. A woman wearing a brown hat and a piece of fur round her throat said with passionate interest, 'May I ask Mr. Dexter if he is engaged on a new work?'

'Oh, yes—yes.'

'May I ask the title?'

'"The Third Man",' Martins said and

gained a spurious confidence as the result of taking that hurdle.

'Mr. Dexter, could you tell us what author has chiefly influenced you?'

Martins, without thinking, said, 'Grey.' He meant of course the author of *Riders of the Purple Sage*, and he was pleased to find his reply gave general satisfaction—to all save an elderly Austrian who asked, 'Grey. What Grey? I do not know the name.'

Martins felt he was safe now and said, 'Zane Grey—I don't know any other,' and was mystified at the low subservient laughter from the English colony.

Crabbin interposed quickly for the sake of the Austrians, 'That is a little joke of Mr. Dexter's. He meant the poet Gray—a gentle, mild, subtle genius—one can see the affinity.'

'And he is called Zane Grey?'

'That was Mr. Dexter's joke. Zane Grey wrote what we call Westerns—cheap popular novelettes about bandits and cowboys.'

'He is not a great writer?'

'No, no. Far from it,' Mr. Crabbin said. 'In the strict sense I would not call him a writer at all.' Martins told me that he felt the first stirrings of revolt at that statement. He had never regarded himself before as a writer, but Crabbin's self-confidence irritated him—

even the way the light flashed back from Crabbin's spectacles seemed an added cause of vexation. Crabbin said, 'He was just a popular entertainer.'

'Why the hell not?' Martins said fiercely.

'Oh, well, I merely meant—'

'What was Shakespeare?'

Somebody with great daring said, 'A poet.'

'Have you ever read Zane Grey?'

'No, I can't say—'

'Then you don't know what you are talking about.'

One of the young men tried to come to Crabbin's rescue. 'And James Joyce, where would you put James Joyce, Mr. Dexter?'

'What do you mean put? I don't want to put anybody anywhere,' Martins said. It had been a very full day: he had drunk too much with Colonel Cooler; he had fallen in love; a man had been murdered—and now he had the quite unjust feeling that he was being got at. Zane Grey was one of his heroes: he was damned if he was going to stand any non-sense.

'I mean would you put him among the really great?'

'If you want to know, I've never heard of him. What did he write?'

He didn't realise it, but he was making an

enormous impression. Only a great writer could have taken so arrogant, so original a line. Several people wrote Zane Grey's name on the backs of envelopes and the Gräfin whispered hoarsely to Crabbin, 'How do you spell Zane?'

'To tell you the truth, I'm not quite sure.'

A number of names were simultaneously flung at Martins—little sharp pointed names like Stein, round pebbles like Woolf. A young Austrian with an intellectual black forelock called out, 'Daphne du Maurier,' and Mr. Crabbin winced and looked sideways at Martins. He said in an undertone, 'Be gentle with them.'

A kind-faced woman in a hand-knitted jumper said wistfully, 'Don't you agree, Mr. Dexter, that no one, no one has written about *feelings* so poetically as Virginia Woolf? In prose, I mean.'

Crabbin whispered, 'You might say something about the stream of consciousness.'

'Stream of what?'

A note of despair came into Crabbin's voice. 'Please, Mr. Dexter, these people are your genuine admirers. They want to hear your views. If you knew how they have *besieged* the Society.'

An elderly Austrian said, 'Is there any

writer in England today of the stature of the late John Galsworthy?'

There was an outburst of angry twittering in which the names of du Maurier, Priestley, and somebody called Layman were flung to and fro. Martins sat gloomily back and saw again the snow, the stretcher, the desperate face of Frau Koch. He thought: if I had never returned, if I had never asked questions, would that little man still be alive? How had he benefited Harry by supplying another victim—a victim to assuage the fear of whom?—Herr Kurtz, Colonel Cooler (he could not believe that), Dr. Winkler? Not one of them seemed adequate to the drab gruesome crime in the basement; he could hear the child saying, 'I saw blood on the coke,' and somebody turned towards him a blank face without features, a grey plasticine egg, the third man.

Martins could not have said how he got through the rest of the discussion: perhaps Crabbin took the brunt; perhaps he was helped by some of the audience who got into an animated discussion about the film version of a popular American novel. He remembered very little more before Crabbin was making a final speech in his honour. Then one of the young men led him to a table stacked with books and asked him to sign them. 'We have only allowed each member one book.'

'What have I got to do?'

'Just a signature. That's all they expect. This is my copy of *The Curved Prow*. I would be so grateful if you'd just write a little something . . .'

Martins took his pen and wrote: 'From B. Dexter, author of *The Lone Rider of Santa Fé*,' and the young man read the sentence and blotted it with a puzzled expression. As Martins sat down and started signing Benjamin Dexter's title pages, he could see in a mirror the young man showing the inscription to Crabbin. Crabbin smiled weakly and stroked his chin, up and down, up and down. 'B. Dexter, B. Dexter, B. Dexter,' Martins wrote rapidly—it was not, after all, a lie. One by one the books were collected by their owners; little half-sentences of delight and compliment were dropped like curtsies—was this what it was to be a writer? Martins began to feel distinct irritation towards Benjamin Dexter. The complacent, tiring, pompous ass, he thought, signing the twenty-seventh copy of *The Curved Prow*. Every time he looked up and took another book he saw Crabbin's worried speculative gaze. The members of the Institute were beginning to go home with their spoils: the room was emptying. Suddenly in the mirror Martins saw a military policeman. He seemed to be having an argument with one of Crabbin's young henchmen. Martins thought he caught the sound of his own name. It was then he lost his nerve and with it any relic of common sense. There was only one book left to sign; he dashed off a last 'B. Dexter' and made for the door. The young man, Crabbin, and the policeman stood together at the entrance.

'And this gentleman?' the policeman asked.

'It's Mr. Benjamin Dexter,' the young man said.

'Lavatory. Is there a lavatory?' Martins said.

'I understood a Mr. Rollo Martins came here in one of your cars.'

'A mistake. An obvious mistake.'

'Second door on the left,' the young man said.

Martins grabbed his coat from the cloak-room as he went and made down the stairs. On the first-floor landing he heard someone mounting the stairs and, looking over, saw Paine, whom I had sent to identify him. He opened a door at random and shut it behind him. He could hear Paine going by. The room where he stood was in darkness; a curious

89

moaning sound made him turn and face whatever room it was.

He could see nothing and the sound had stopped. He made a tiny movement and once more it started, like an impeded breath. He remained still and the sound died away. Outside somebody called, 'Mr. Dexter, Mr. Dexter.' Then a new sound started. It was like somebody whispering—a long continuous monologue in the darkness. Martins said, 'Is anybody there?' and the sound stopped again. He could stand no more of it. He took out his lighter. Footsteps went by and down the stairs. He scraped and scraped at the little wheel and no light came. Somebody shifted in the dark, and something rattled in mid-air like a chain. He asked once more with the anger of fear, 'Is anybody there?' and only the click-click of metal answered him.

Martins felt desperately for a light switch, first to his right hand and then to his left. He did not dare go farther because he could no longer locate his fellow occupant; the whisper, the moaning, the click had all stopped. Then he was afraid that he had lost the door and felt wildly for the knob. He was far less afraid of the police than he was of the darkness, and he had no idea of the noise he was making.

Paine heard it from the bottom of the stairs and came back. He switched on the landing light, and the glow under the door gave Martins his direction. He opened the door and, smiling weakly at Paine, turned back to take a second look at the room. The eyes of a parrot chained to a perch stared beadily back at him. Paine said respectfully, 'We were looking for you, sir. Colonel Calloway wants a word with you.'

'I lost my way,' Martins said.

'Yes, sir. We thought that was what had happened.'

# CHAPTER TEN

I HAD kept a very careful record of Martins' movements from the moment I knew that he had not caught the plane home. He had been seen with Kurtz, and at the Josefstadt Theatre; I knew about his visit to Dr. Winkler and to Colonel Cooler, his first return to the block where Harry had lived. For some reason my man lost him between Cooler's and Anna Schmidt's flats; he reported that Martins had wandered widely, and the impression we both got was that he had deliberately thrown off his shadower. I tried to pick him up at the hotel and just missed him.

Events had taken a disquieting turn, and it seemed to me that the time had come for another interview. He had a lot to explain.

I put a good wide desk between us and gave him a cigarette. I found him sullen but ready to talk, within strict limits. I asked him about Kurtz and he seemed to me to answer satisfactorily. I then asked him about Anna Schmidt and I gathered from his reply that he must have been with her after visiting Colonel Cooler; that filled in one of the missing points. I tried him with Dr. Winkler, and he answered readily enough. 'You've been getting around,' I said, 'quite a bit. And have you found out anything about your friend?'

'Oh, yes,' he said. 'It was under your nose but you didn't see it.'

'What?'

'That he was murdered.' That took me by surprise: I had at one time played with the idea of suicide, but I had ruled even that out.

'Go on,' I said. He tried to eliminate from his story all mention of Koch, talking about an informant who had seen the accident. This made his story rather confusing, and I couldn't grasp at first why he attached so much importance to the third man.

'He didn't turn up at the inquest, and the others lied to keep him out.'

'Nor did your man turn up—I don't see much importance in that. If it was a genuine accident, all the evidence needed was there. Why get the other chap in trouble? Perhaps his wife thought he was out of town; perhaps he was an official absent without leave—people sometimes take unauthorised trips to Vienna from places like Klagenfurt. The delights of the great city, for what they are worth.'

'There was more to it than that. The little chap who told me about it—they've murdered him. You see, they obviously didn't know what else he had seen.'

'Now we have it,' I said. 'You mean Koch.'

'Yes.'

'As far as we know, you were the last person to see him alive.' I questioned him then, as I've written, to find out if he had been followed to Koch's by somebody who was sharper than my man and had kept out of sight. I said, 'The Austrian police are anxious to pin this on you. Frau Koch told them how disturbed her husband was by your visit. Who else knew about it?'

'I told Cooler.' He said excitedly, 'Suppose immediately I left he telephoned the story to someone—to the third man. They had to stop Koch's mouth.'

'When you told Colonel Cooler about Koch, the man was already dead. That night he got out of bed, hearing someone, and went downstairs—'

'Well, that rules me out. I was in Sacher's.'

'But he went to bed very early. Your visit brought back the migraine. It was soon after nine that he got up. You returned to Sacher's at nine-thirty. Where were you before that?'

He said gloomily, 'Wandering round and trying to sort things out.'

'Any evidence of your movements?'

'No.'

I wanted to frighten him, so there was no point in telling him that he had been followed all the time. I knew that he hadn't cut Koch's throat, but I wasn't sure that he was quite so innocent as he made out. The man who owns the knife is not always the real murderer.

'Can I have a cigarette?'

'Yes.'

He said, 'How did you know that I went to Koch's? That was why you pulled me here, wasn't it?'

'The Austrian police—'

'They hadn't identified me.'

'Immediately you left Colonel Cooler's, he telephoned to me.'

'Then that lets him out. If he had been concerned, he wouldn't have wanted me to tell you my story—to tell Koch's story, I mean.'

'He might assume that you were a sensible man and would come to me with your story as soon as you learned of Koch's death. By the way, how did you learn of it?'

He told me promptly and I believed him. It was then I began to believe him altogether. He said, 'I still can't believe Cooler's concerned. I'd stake anything on his honesty. He's one of those Americans with a real sense of duty.'

'Yes,' I said, 'he told me about that when he phoned. He apologised for it. He said it was the worst of having been brought up to believe in citizenship. He said it made him feel a prig. To tell you the truth, Cooler irritates me. Of course he doesn't know that I know about his type deals.'

'Is he in a racket, too, then?'

'Not a very serious one. I daresay he's salted away twenty-five thousand dollars. But I'm not a good citizen. Let the Americans look after their own people.'

'I'm damned.' He said thoughtfully, 'Is that the kind of thing Harry was up to?'

'No. It was not so harmless.'

He said, 'You know this business—Koch's death—has shaken me. Perhaps Harry did get mixed up in something bad. Perhaps he was trying to clear out again, and that's why they murdered him.'

'Or perhaps,' I said, 'they wanted a bigger cut off the spoils. Thieves fall out.'

He took it this time without any anger at all. He said, 'We won't agree about motives, but I think you check your facts pretty well. I'm sorry about the other day.'

'That's all right.' There are times when one has to make a flash decision—this was one of them. I owed him something in return for the

96

information he had given me. I said, 'I'll show you enough of the facts in Lime's case for you to understand. But don't fly off the handle. It's going to be a shock.'

It couldn't help being a shock. The war and the peace (if you can call it peace) let loose a great number of rackets, but none more vile than this one. The black marketeers in food did at least supply food, and the same applied to all the other racketeers who provided articles in short supply at extravagant prices. But the penicillin racket was a different affair altogether. Penicillin in Austria was supplied only to the military hospitals; no civilian doctor, not even a civilian hospital, could obtain it by legal means. As the racket started, it was relatively harmless. Penicillin would be stolen by military orderlies and sold to Austrian doctors for very high sums—a phial would fetch anything up to seventy pounds. You might say that this was a form of distribution—unfair distribution because it benefited only the rich patient, but the original distribution could hardly have a claim to greater fairness.

This racket went on quite happily for a while. Occasionally an orderly was caught and punished, but the danger simply raised the price of penicillin. Then the racket began to get organised: the big men saw big money in it, and while the original thief got less for his spoils, he received instead a certain security. If anything happened to him he would be looked after. Human nature too has curious twisted reasons that the heart certainly knows nothing of. It eased the conscience of many small men to feel that they were working for an employer: they were almost as respectable soon in their own eyes as wage-earners; they were one of a group, and if there was guilt, the leaders bore the guilt. A racket works very like a totalitarian party.

This I have sometimes called stage two. Stage three was when the organisers decided that the profits were not large enough. Penicillin would not always be impossible to obtain legitimately; they wanted more money and quicker money while the going was good. They began to dilute the penicillin with coloured water, and, in the case of pencillin dust, with sand. I keep a small museum in one drawer in my desk, and I showed Martins examples. He wasn't enjoying the talk, but he hadn't yet grasped the point. He said, 'I suppose that makes the stuff useless.'

I said, 'We wouldn't worry so much if that was all, but just consider. You can be immunised from the effects of pencillin. At the best you can say that the use of this stuff makes a penicillin treatment for the particular patient ineffective in the future. That isn't so funny, of course, if you are suffering from V.D. Then the use of sand on a wound that requires penicillin—well, it's not healthy. Men have lost their legs and arms that way—and their lives. But perhaps what horrified me most was visiting the children's hospital here. They had bought some of this penicillin for use against meningitis. A number of children simply died, and a number went off their heads. You can see them now in the mental ward.'

He sat on the other side of the desk, scowling into his hands. I said, 'It doesn't bear thinking about very closely, does it?'

'You haven't showed me any evidence yet that Harry—'

'We are coming to that now,' I said. 'Just sit still and listen.' I opened Lime's file and began to read. At the beginning the evidence was purely circumstantial, and Martins fidgeted. So much consisted of coincidence—reports of agents that Lime had been at a certain place at a certain time; the accumulation of opportunities; his acquaintance with certain people. He protested once, 'But the same evidence would apply against me—now.'

'Just wait,' I said. For some reason Harry Lime had grown careless: he may have realised that we suspected him and got rattled. He held a quite distinguished position in the Relief Organisation, and a man like that is the more easily rattled. We put one of our agents as an orderly in the British Military Hospital: we knew by this time the name of our go-between, but we had never succeeded in getting the line right back to the source. Anyway, I am not going to bother the reader now, as I bothered Martins then, with all the stages—the long tussle to win the confidence of the go-between, a man called Harbin. At last we had the screws on Harbin, and we twisted them until he squealed. This kind of police work is very similar to secret service work: you look for a double agent whom you can really control, and Harbin was the man for us. But even he only led us as far as Kurtz.

'Kurtz!' Martins exclaimed. 'But why haven't you pulled him in?'

'Zero hour is almost here,' I said.

Kurtz was a great step forward, for Kurtz was in direct communication with Lime—he had a small outside job in connection with international relief. With Kurtz, Lime sometimes put things on paper—if he was pressed. I showed Martins the photostat of a note.

'Can you identify that?'

'It's Harry's hand.' He read it through. 'I don't see anything wrong.'

'No, but now read this note from Harbin to Kurtz—which we dictated. Look at the date. This is the result.'

He read them both through twice.

'You see what I mean?' If one watched a world come to an end, a plane dive from its course, I don't suppose one would chatter, and a world for Martins had certainly come to an end, a world of easy friendship, hero-worship, confidence that had begun twenty years before—in a school corridor. Every memory—afternoons in the long grass, the illegitimate shoots on Brickworth Common, the dreams, the walks, every shared experience was simultaneously tainted, like the soil of an atomised town. One could not walk there with safety for a long while. While he sat there, looking at his hands and saying nothing, I fetched a precious bottle of whisky out of a cupboard and poured out two large doubles. 'Go on,' I said, 'drink that,' and he obeyed me as though I were his doctor. I poured him out another.

He said slowly, 'Are you certain that he was the real boss?'

'It's as far back as we have got so far.'

'You see, he was always apt to jump before he looked.'

I didn't contradict him, though that wasn't the impression he had before given of Lime. He was searching round for some comfort.

'Suppose,' he said, 'someone had got a line on him, forced him into this racket, as you forced Harbin to double-cross . . .'

'It's possible.'

'And they murdered him in case he talked when he was arrested.'

'It's not impossible.'

'I'm glad they did,' he said. 'I wouldn't have liked to hear Harry squeal.' He made a curious little dusting movement with his hand on his knee as much as to say, 'That's that.' He said, 'I'll be getting back to England.'

'I'd rather you didn't just yet. The Austrian police would make an issue if you tried to leave Vienna at the moment. You see, Cooler's sense of duty made him call them up too.'

'I see,' he said hopelessly.

'When we've found the third man . . .' I said.

'I'd like to hear *him* squeal,' he said. 'The bastard. The bloody bastard.'

# CHAPTER ELEVEN

AFTER he left me, Martins went straight off to drink himself silly. He chose the Oriental to do it in, the dreary smoky little night club that stands behind a sham Eastern façade. The same semi-nude photographs on the stairs, the same half-drunk Americans at the bar, the same bad wine and extraordinary gins—he might have been in any third-rate night haunt in any other shabby capital of a shabby Europe. At one point of the hopeless early hours the International Patrol took a look at the scene, and a Russian soldier made a bolt for the stairs at the sight of them, moving with bent averted head like a small harvest animal. The Americans never stirred and nobody interfered with them. Martins had drink after drink; he would probably have had a woman too, but the cabaret performers had all gone home, and there were practically no women left in the place, except for one beautiful shrewd-looking French journalist who made one remark to her companion and fell contemptuously asleep.

Martins moved on: at Maxim's a few couples were dancing rather gloomily, and at a place called Chez Victor the heating had failed and people sat in overcoats drinking cocktails. By this time the spots were swimming in front of Martins' eyes, and he was oppressed by a sense of loneliness. His mind reverted to the girl in Dublin, and the one in Amsterdam. That was one thing that didn't fool you—the straight drink, the simple physical act: one didn't expect fidelity from a woman. His mind revolved in circles—from sentiment to lust and back again from belief to cynicism.

The trams had stopped, and he set out obstinately on foot to find Harry's girl. He wanted to make love to her—just like that: no nonsense, no sentiment. He was in the mood for violence, and the snowy road heaved like a lake and set his mind on a new course towards sorrow, eternal love, renunciation. In the corner of a sheltering wall he was sick in the snow.

It must have been about three in the morning when he climbed the stairs to Anna's room. He was nearly sober by that time and had only one idea in his head, that she must know about Harry too. He felt that somehow this knowledge would pay the mortmain that memory levies on human beings, and he would stand a chance with Harry's girl. If you are in love yourself, it never occurs to you that the girl doesn't know: you believe you have told it plainly in a tone of voice, the touch of a hand. When Anna opened the door to him, with astonishment at the sight of him tousled on the threshold, he never imagined that she was opening the door to a stranger.

He said, 'Anna, I've found out everything.'

'Come in,' she said, 'you don't want to wake the house.' She was in a dressing-gown; the divan had become a bed, the kind of tumbled bed that showed how sleepless the occupant had been.

'Now,' she said, while he stood there, fumbling for words, 'what is it? I thought you were going to keep away. Are the police after you?'

'No.'

'You didn't really kill that man, did you?'

'Of course not.'

'You're drunk, aren't you?'

'I am a bit,' he said sulkily. The meeting seemed to be going on the wrong lines. He said angrily, 'I'm sorry.'

'Why? I would like a drink myself.'

He said, 'I've been with the British police. They are satisfied I didn't do it. But I've learned everything from them. Harry was in a racket—a bad racket.' He said hopelessly,

105

'He was no good at all. We were both wrong.'

'You'd better tell me,' Anna said. She sat down on the bed and he told her, swaying slightly beside the table where her typescript part still lay open at the first page. I imagine he told it to her pretty confusedly, dwelling chiefly on what had struck most in his mind, the children dead with meningitis and the children in the mental ward. He stopped and they were silent. She said, 'Is that all?'

'Yes.'

'You were sober when they told you? They really proved it?'

'Yes.' He added drearily, 'So that, you see, was Harry.'

'I'm glad he's dead now,' she said. 'I wouldn't have wanted him to rot for years in prison.'

'But can you understand how Harry— your Harry, my Harry—could have got mixed up . . .?' He said hopelessly, 'I feel as though he had never really existed, that we'd dreamed him. Was he laughing at fools like us all the time?'

'He may have been. What does it matter?' she said. 'Sit down. Don't worry.' He had pictured himself comforting *her*—not this other way about. She said, 'If he was alive now, he might be able to explain, but we've got to remember him as he was to us. There are always so many things one doesn't know about a person, even a person one loves— good things, bad things. We have to leave plenty of room for them.'

'Those children—'

She said angrily, 'For God's sake stop making people in *your* image. Harry was real. He wasn't just your hero and my lover. He was Harry. He was in a racket. He did bad things. What about it? He was the man we knew.'

He said, 'Don't talk such bloody wisdom. Don't you see that I love you?'

She looked at him in astonishment. 'You?'

'Yes, me. I don't kill people with fake drugs. I'm not a hypocrite who persuades people that I'm the greatest—I'm just a bad writer who drinks too much and falls in love with girls . . .'

She said, 'But I don't even know what colour your eyes are. If you'd rung me up just now and asked me whether you were dark or fair or wore a moustache, I wouldn't have known.'

'Can't you get him out of your mind?'

'No.'

He said, 'As soon as they've cleared up this Koch murder, I'm leaving Vienna. I can't feel interested any longer in whether Kurtz killed Harry—or the third man. Whoever killed him it was a kind of justice. Maybe I'd kill him myself under these circumstances. But you still love him. You love a cheat, a murderer.'

'I loved a man,' she said. 'I told you—a man doesn't alter because you find out more about him. He's still the same man.'

'I hate the way you talk. I've got a splitting headache, and you talk and talk . . .'

'I didn't ask you to come.'

'You make me cross.'

Suddenly she laughed. She said, 'You are so comic. You come here at three in the morning—a stranger—and say you love me. Then you get angry and pick a quarrel. What do you expect me to do—or say?'

'I haven't seen you laugh before. Do it again. I like it.'

'There isn't enough for two laughs,' she said.

He took her by the shoulders and shook her gently. He said, 'I'd make comic faces all day long. I'd stand on my head and grin at you between my legs. I'd learn a lot of jokes from the books on after-dinner speaking.'

'Come away from the window. There are no curtains.'

'There's nobody to see.' But automatically

checking his statement, he wasn't quite so sure: a long shadow that had moved, perhaps with the movement of clouds over the moon, was motionless again. He said, 'You still love Harry, don't you?'

'Yes.'

'Perhaps I do. I don't know.' He dropped his hands and said, 'I'll be pushing off.'

He walked rapidly away. He didn't bother to see whether he was being followed, to check up on the shadow. But, passing by the end of a street, he happened to turn, and there just around the corner, pressed against a wall to escape notice, was a thick stocky figure. Martins stopped and stared. There was something familiar about that figure. Perhaps, he thought, I have grown unconsciously used to him during these last twenty-four hours; perhaps he is one of those who have so assiduously checked my movements. Martins stood there, twenty yards away, staring at the silent motionless figure in the dark side street who stared back at him. A police spy, perhaps, or an agent of those other men, those men who had corrupted Harry first and then killed him—even possibly the third man?

It was not the face that was familiar, for he could not make out so much as the angle of the jaw; nor a movement, for the body was so still that he began to believe that the whole thing was an illusion caused by shadow. He called sharply, 'Do you want anything?' and there was no reply. He called again with the irascibility of drink, 'Answer, can't you,' and an answer came, for a window curtain was drawn petulantly back by some sleeper he had awakened, and the light fell straight across the narrow street and lit up the features of Harry Lime.

# CHAPTER TWELVE

'Do you believe in ghosts?' Martins said to me.

'Do you?'

'I do now.'

'I also believe that drunk men see things—sometimes rats, sometimes worse.'

He hadn't come to me at once with his story—only the danger to Anna Schmidt tossed him back into my office, like something the sea had washed up, tousled, unshaven, haunted by an experience he couldn't understand. He said, 'If it had been just the face, I wouldn't have worried. I'd been thinking about Harry, and I might easily have mistaken a stranger. The light was turned off again at once, you see. I only got one glimpse, and the man made off down the street—if he was a man. There was no turning for a long way, but I was so startled I gave him another thirty yards' start. He came to one of those newspaper kiosks and for a moment moved out of sight. I ran after him. It only took me ten seconds to reach the kiosk, and he must have heard me running, but the strange thing was he never appeared again. I reached the kiosk. There wasn't anybody there. The street was empty. He couldn't have reached a doorway without my seeing him. He simply vanished.'

'A natural thing for ghosts—or illusions.'

'But I can't believe I was as drunk as all that!'

'What did you do then?'

'I had to have another drink. My nerves were all in pieces.'

'Didn't that bring him back?'

'No, but it sent me back to Anna's.'

I think he would have been ashamed to come to me with his absurd story if it had not been for the attempt on Anna Schmidt. My theory, when he did tell me his story, was that there had been a watcher—though it was drink and hysteria that had pasted on the man's face the features of Harry Lime. The watcher had noted his visit to Anna, and the member of the ring—the penicillin ring—had been warned by telephone. Events that night moved fast. You remember that Kurtz lived in the Russian zone—in the second Bezirk to be exact, in a wide, empty, desolate street that runs down to the Prater Platz. A man like that had probably obtained his influential contacts. It was ruin for a Russian to be observed on very friendly terms with an

American or an Englishman, but the Austrian was a potential ally—and in any case one doesn't fear the influence of the ruined and defeated.

You must understand that at this period co-operation between the Western Allies and the Russians had practically, though not yet completely, broken down.

The original police agreement in Vienna between the Allies confined the military police (who had to deal with crimes involving allied personnel) to their particular zones, unless permission was given to them to enter the zone of another power. This agreement worked well enough between the three Western powers. I only had to get on the phone to my opposite number in the American or French zones before I sent in my men to make an arrest or pursue an investigation. During the first six months of the occupation it had worked reasonably well with the Russians: perhaps forty-eight hours would pass before I received permission, but in practice there are few occasions when it is necessary to work quicker than that. Even at home it is not always possible to obtain a search warrant or permission from one's superiors to detain a suspect with any greater speed. Then the forty-eight hours turned into a week or a fortnight, and I remember my American colleague suddenly taking a look at his records and discovering that there were forty cases dating back more than three months where not even an acknowledgment of his requests had been received. Then the trouble started. We began to turn down, or not to answer, the Russian requests, and sometimes without permission they would send in police, and there were clashes. . . . At the date of this story the Western powers had more or less ceased to put in applications or reply to the Russian ones. This meant that if I wanted to pick up Kurtz it would be as well to catch him outside the Russian zone, though of course it was always possible his activities might offend the Russians and his punishment be more sudden and severe than any we should inflict. Well, the Anna Schmidt case was one of the clashes: when Rollo Martins went drunkenly back at four o'clock in the morning to tell Anna that he had seen the ghost of Harry, he was told by a frightened porter who had not yet gone back to sleep that she had been taken away by the International Patrol.

What happened was this. Russia, you remember, was in the chair as far as the Inner Stadt was concerned, and when Russia was in the chair, you expected certain irregularities. On this occasion, half way through the patrol the Russian policeman pulled a fast one on his colleagues and directed the car to the street where Anna Schmidt lived. The British military policeman that night was new to his job: he didn't realise, till his colleagues told him, that they had entered a British zone. He spoke a little German and no French, and the Frenchman, a cynical hard-bitten Parisian, gave up the attempt to explain to him. The American took on the job. 'It's all right by me,' he said, 'but is it all right by you?' The British M.P. tapped the Russian's shoulder, who turned his Mongol face and launched a flood of incomprehensible Slav at him. The car drove on.

Outside Anna Schmidt's block the American took a hand in the game and demanded in German what it was all about. The Frenchman leaned against the bonnet and lit a stinking Caporal. France wasn't concerned, and anything that didn't concern France had no genuine importance to him. The Russian dug out a few words of German and flourished some papers. As far as they could tell, a Russian national wanted by the Russian police was living there without proper papers. They went upstairs and the Russian tried

Anna's door. It was firmly bolted, but he put his shoulder to it and tore out the bolt without giving the occupant an opportunity of letting him in. Anna was in bed, though I don't suppose, after Martins' visit, that she was asleep.

There is a lot of comedy in these situations if you are not directly concerned. You need a background of Central European terror, of a father who belonged to a losing side, of house searches and disappearances, before the fear outweighed the comedy. The Russian, you see, refused to leave the room while Anna dressed: the Englishman refused to remain in the room: the American wouldn't leave a girl unprotected with a Russian soldier, and the Frenchman—well, I think the Frenchman must have thought it was fun. Can't you imagine the scene? The Russian was just doing his duty and watched the girl all the time, without a flicker of sexual interest; the American stood with his back chivalrously turned, but aware, I am sure, of every movement; the Frenchman smoked his cigarette and watched with detached amusement the reflection of the girl dressing in the mirror of the wardrobe; and the Englishman stood in the passage wondering what to do next.

I don't want you to think the English policeman came too badly out of the affair. In the passage, undistracted by chivalry, he had time to think, and his thoughts led him to the telephone in the next flat. He got straight through to me at my flat and woke me out of that deepest middle sleep. That was why when Martins rang up an hour later I already knew what was exciting him; it gave him an undeserved but very useful belief in my efficiency. I never had another crack from him about policemen or sheriffs after that night.

I must explain another point of police procedure. If the International Patrol made an arrest, they had to lodge their prisoner for twenty-four hours at the International Headquarters. During that period it would be determined which power could justifiably claim the prisoner. It was this rule that the Russians were most ready to break. Because so few of us can speak Russian and the Russian is almost debarred from explaining his point of view (try and explain your own point of view on any subject in a language you don't know well—it's not as easy as ordering a meal), we are apt to regard any breach of an agreement by the Russians as deliberate and malign. I think it quite possible that they understood this agreement as referring only to prisoners about whom there was a dispute. It's true that there was a dispute about nearly every prisoner they took, but there was no dispute in their own minds, and no one has a greater sense of self-righteousness than a Russian. Even in his confessions a Russian is self-righteous—he pours out his revelations, but he doesn't excuse himself, he needs no excuse. All this had to form the background of one's decision. I gave my instructions to Corporal Starling.

When he went back to Anna's room a dispute was raging. Anna had told the American that she had Austrian papers (which was true) and that they were quite in order (which was rather stretching the truth). The American told the Russian in bad German that they had no right to arrest an Austrian citizen. He asked Anna for her papers and when she produced them, the Russian snatched them from her hand.

'Hungarian,' he said, pointing at Anna. 'Hungarian,' and then, flourishing the papers, 'bad, bad.'

The American, whose name was O'Brien, said, 'Give the goil back her papers,' which the Russian naturally didn't understand. The American put his hand on his gun, and Corporal Starling said gently, 'Let it go, Pat.'

'If those papers ain't in order we got a right to look.'

'Just let it go. We'll see the papers at HQ.'

'If we get to HQ. You can't trust these Russian drivers. As like as not he'll drive straight through to the second Bezirk.'

'We'll see,' Starling said.

'The trouble about you British is you never know when to make a stand.'

'Oh, well,' Starling said; he had been at Dunkirk, but he knew when to be quiet.

They got back into the car with Anna, who sat in the front between the two Russians dumb with fear. After they had gone a little way the American touched the Russian on the shoulder, 'Wrong way,' he said. 'HQ that way.' The Russian chattered back in his own tongue making a conciliatory gesture, while they drove on. 'It's what I said,' O'Brien told Starling. 'They are taking her to the Russian zone.' Anna stared out with terror through the windscreen. 'Don't worry, little goil,' O'Brien said, 'I'll fix them all right.' His hand was fidgeting round his gun again. Starling said, 'Look here, Pat, this is a British case. You don't have to get involved.'

'You are new to this game. You don't know these bastards.'

'It's not worth making an incident about.'

'For Christ's sake,' O'Brien said, 'not

worth . . . that little goil's got to have protection.' American chivalry is always, it seems to me, carefully canalised—one still awaits the American saint who will kiss a leper's sores.

The driver put on his brakes suddenly: there was a road block. You see, I knew they would have to pass this military post if they did not make their way to the International HQ in the Inner City. I put my head in at the window and said to the Russian haltingly, in his own tongue, 'What are you doing in the British zone?'

He grumbled that it was 'orders'.

'Whose orders? Let me see them.' I noted the signature—it was useful information. I said, 'This tells you to pick up a certain Hungarian national and war criminal who is living with faulty papers in the British zone. Let me see the papers.'

He started on a long explanation, but I saw the papers sticking in his pocket and I pulled them out. He made a grab at his gun, and I punched his face—I felt really mean at doing so, but it's the conduct they expect from an angry officer and it brought him to reason—that and seeing three British soldiers approaching his headlights. I said, 'These papers look to me quite in order, but

I'll investigate them and send a report of the result to your colonel. He can, of course, ask for the extradition of this lady at any time. All we want is proof of her criminal activities. I'm afraid we don't regard Hungarian in itself as Russian nationality.' He giggled at me (my Russian was probably half incomprehensible) and I said to Anna, 'Get out of the car.' She couldn't get by the Russian, so I had to pull him out first. Then I put a packet of cigarettes in his hand, said, 'Have a good smoke,' waved my hand to the others, gave a sigh of relief, and that incident was closed.

# CHAPTER THIRTEEN

WHILE Martins told me how he went back to Anna's and found her gone, I did some hard thinking. I wasn't satisfied with the ghost story or the idea that the man with Harry Lime's features had been a drunken illusion. I took out two maps of Vienna and compared them. I rang up my assistant and, keeping Martins silent with a glass of whisky, asked him if he had located Harbin yet. He said no; he understood he'd left Klagenfurt a week ago to visit his family in the adjoining zone. One always wants to do everything oneself; one has to guard against blaming one's juniors. I am convinced that I would never have let Harbin out of our clutches, but then I would probably have made all kinds of mistakes that my junior would have avoided. 'All right,' I said. 'Go on trying to get hold of him.'

'I'm sorry, sir.'

'Forget it. It's just one of those things.'

His young enthusiastic voice—if only one could still feel that enthusiasm for a routine job; how many opportunities, flashes of insight one misses simply because a job has become just a job—tingled up the wire. 'You know, sir, I can't help feeling that we ruled out the possibility of murder too easily. There are one or two points—'

'Put them on paper, Carter.'

'Yes, sir. I think, sir, if you don't mind my saying so' (Carter is a very young man), 'we ought to have him dug up. There's no real evidence that he died just when the others said.'

'I agree, Carter. Get on to the authorities.'

Martins was right. I had made a complete fool of myself, but remember that police work in an occupied city is not like police work at home. Everything is unfamiliar: the methods of one's foreign colleagues, the rules of evidence, even the procedure at inquests. I suppose I had got into the state of mind when one trusts too much to one's personal judgment. I had been immensely relieved by Lime's death. I was satisfied with the accident.

I said to Martins, 'Did you look inside the newspaper kiosk or was it locked?'

'Oh, it wasn't exactly a newspaper kiosk,' he said. 'It was one of those solid iron kiosks you see everywhere plastered with posters.'

'You'd better show me the place.'

'But is Anna all right?'

'The police are watching the flat. They won't try anything else yet.'

I didn't want to make a fuss and stir in the

neighbourhood with a police car, so we took trams—several trams—changing here and there, and came into the district on foot. I didn't wear my uniform, and I doubted anyway, after the failure of the attempt on Anna, whether they would risk a watcher. 'This is the turning,' Martins said and led me down a side street. We stopped at the kiosk. 'You see, he passed behind here and simply vanished—into the ground.'

'That was exactly where he did vanish to,' I said.

'How do you mean?'

An ordinary passer-by would never have noticed that the kiosk had a door, and of course it had been dark when the man disappeared. I pulled the door open and showed Martins the little curling iron staircase that disappeared into the ground. He said, 'Good God, then I didn't imagine him!'

'It's one of the entrances to the main sewer.'

'And anyone can go down?'

'Anyone. For some reason the Russians object to these being locked.'

'How far can one go?'

'Right across Vienna. People used them in air raids; some of our prisoners hid for two years down there. Deserters have used them—and burglars. If you know your way about you can emerge again almost anywhere in the city through a manhole or a kiosk like this one. The Austrians have to have special police for patrolling these sewers.' I closed the door of the kiosk again. I said, 'So that's how your friend Harry disappeared.'

'You really believe it was Harry?'

'The evidence points that way.'

'Then whom did they bury?'

'I don't know yet, but we soon shall, because we are digging him up again. I've got a shrewd idea, though, that Koch wasn't the only inconvenient man they murdered.'

Martins said, 'It's a bit of a shock.'

'Yes.'

'What are you going to do about it?'

'I don't know. It's no good applying to the Russians, and you can bet he's hiding out now in the Russian zone. We have no line now on Kurtz, for Harbin's blown—he must have been blown or they wouldn't have staged that mock death and funeral.'

'But it's odd, isn't it, that Koch didn't recognise the dead man's face from the window?'

'The window was a long way up and I expect the face had been damaged before they took the body out of the car.'

He said thoughtfully, 'I wish I could speak

to him. You see, there's so much I simply can't believe.'

'Perhaps you are the only one who could speak to him. It's risky enough, because you know too much.'

'I still can't believe—I only saw the face for a moment.' He said, 'What shall I do?'

'He won't leave the Russian zone now. Perhaps that's why he tried to have the girl taken over—because he loves her? because he doesn't feel secure? I don't know. I do know that the only person who could persuade him to come over would be you—or her, if he still believes you are his friend. But first you've got to speak to him. I can't see the line.'

'I could go and see Kurtz. I have the address.'

I said, 'Remember. Lime may not want you to leave the Russian zone when once you are there, and I can't protect you there.'

'I want to clear the whole damned thing up,' Martins said, 'but I'm not going to act as a decoy. I'll talk to him. That's all.'

# CHAPTER FOURTEEN

SUNDAY had laid its false peace over Vienna; the wind had dropped and no snow had fallen for twenty-four hours. All the morning trams had been full, going out to Grinzing where the young wine was drunk and to the slopes of snow on the hills outside. Walking over the canal by the makeshift military bridge, Martins was aware of the emptiness of the afternoon: the young were out with their toboggans and their skis, and all around him was the after-dinner sleep of age. A notice board told him that he was entering the Russian zone, but there were no signs of occupation. You saw more Russian soldiers in the Inner City than here.

Deliberately he had given Mr. Kurtz no warning of his visit. Better to find him out than a reception prepared for him. He was careful to carry with him all his papers, including the laissez-passer of the four powers that on the face of it allowed him to move freely through all the zones of Vienna. It was extraordinarily quiet over here on the other side of the canal, and a melodramatic journalist had painted a picture of silent terror, but the truth was simply the wider streets, the greater shell damage, the fewer people—and Sunday afternoon. There was nothing to fear, but all the same, in this huge empty street where all the time you heard your own feet moving, it was difficult not to look behind.

He had no difficulty in finding Mr. Kurtz' block, and when he rang the bell the door was opened quickly, as though Mr. Kurtz expected a visitor, by Mr. Kurtz himself.

'Oh,' Mr. Kurtz said, 'it's you, Mr. Martins,' and made a perplexed motion with his hand to the back of his head. Martins had been wondering why he looked so different, and now he knew. Mr. Kurtz was not wearing the toupée, and yet his head was not bald. He had a perfectly normal head of hair cut close. He said, 'It would have been better to have telephoned to me. You nearly missed me; I was going out.'

'May I come in a moment?'

'Of course.'

In the hall a cupboard door stood open, and Martins saw Mr. Kurtz' overcoat, his raincoat, a couple of soft hats, and, hanging sedately on a peg like a wrap, Mr. Kurtz' toupée. He said, 'I'm glad to see your hair has grown,' and was astonished to see, in the mirror on the cupboard door, the hatred flame and blush on Mr. Kurtz' face. When he turned Mr. Kurtz smiled at him like a conspirator and said vaguely, 'It keeps the head warm.'

'Whose head?' Martins asked, for it had suddenly occurred to him how useful that toupée might have been on the day of the accident. 'Never mind,' he went quickly on, for his errand was not with Mr. Kurtz. 'I'm here to see Harry.'

'Harry?'

'I want to talk to him.'

'Are you mad?'

'I'm in a hurry, so let's assume that I am. Just make a note of my madness. If you should see Harry—or his ghost—let him know that I want to talk to him. A ghost isn't afraid of a man, is it? Surely it's the other way round. I'll be waiting in the Prater by the Big Wheel for the next two hours—if you can get in touch with the dead, hurry.' He added, 'Remember, I was Harry's friend.'

Kurtz said nothing, but somewhere, in a room off the hall, somebody cleared his throat. Martins threw open a door; he had half expected to see the dead rise yet again, but it was only Dr. Winkler who rose from a kitchen chair, in front of the kitchen stove, and bowed very stiffly and correctly with the same celluloid squeak.

'Dr. Winkle,' Martins said. Dr. Winkler looked extraordinarily out of place in a kitchen. The debris of a snack lunch littered the kitchen table, and the unwashed dishes consorted very ill with Dr. Winkler's cleanness.

'Winkler,' the doctor corrected him with stony patience.

Martins said to Kurtz, 'Tell the doctor about my madness. He might be able to make a diagnosis. And remember the place—by the Great Wheel. Or do ghosts only rise by night?' He left the flat.

For an hour he waited, walking up and down to keep warm, inside the enclosure of the Great Wheel; the smashed Prater with its bones sticking crudely through the snow was nearly empty. One stall sold thin flat cakes like cartwheels, and the children queued with their coupons. A few courting couples would be packed together in a single car of the Wheel and revolve slowly above the city, surrounded by empty cars. As the car reached the highest point of the Wheel, the revolutions would stop for a couple of minutes and far overhead the tiny faces would press against the glass. Martins wondered who would come for him. Was there enough friendship left in Harry for him to come alone, or would a squad of police arrive? It was obvious from the raid on Anna Schmidt's flat that he had a certain pull. And then as his watch hand passed the hour, he wondered: Was it all an invention of my mind? are they digging up Harry's body now in the Central Cemetery?

Somewhere behind the cake stall a man was whistling, and Martins knew the tune. He turned and waited. Was it fear or excitement that made his heart beat—or just the memories that tune ushered in, for life had always quickened when Harry came, came just as he came now, as though nothing much had happened, nobody had been lowered into a grave or found with cut throat in a basement, came with his amused deprecating take-it-or-leave-it manner—and of course one always took it.

'Harry.'

'Hullo, Rollo.'

Don't picture Harry Lime as a smooth scoundrel. He wasn't that. The picture I have of him on my files is an excellent one: he is caught by a street photographer with his stocky legs apart, big shoulders a little hunched, a belly that has known too much good food for too long, on his face a look of cheerful rascality, a geniality, a recognition that *his* happiness will make the world's day. Now he didn't make the mistake of putting out a hand that might have been rejected, but instead just patted Martins on the elbow and said, 'How are things?'

'We've got to talk, Harry.'

'Of course.'

'Alone.'

'We couldn't be more alone than here.'

He had always known the ropes, and even in the smashed pleasure park he knew them, tipping the woman in charge of the Wheel, so that they might have a car to themselves. He said, 'Lovers used to do this in the old days, but they haven't the money to spare, poor devils, now,' and he looked out of the window of the swaying, rising car at the figures diminishing below with what looked like genuine commiseration.

Very slowly on one side of them the city sank; very slowly on the other the great cross-girders of the Wheel rose into sight. As the horizon slid away the Danube became visible, and the piers of the Kaiser Friedrich Brücke lifted above the houses. 'Well,' Harry said, 'it's good to see you, Rollo.'

'I was at your funeral.'

'That was pretty smart of me, wasn't it?'

'Not so smart for your girl. She was there too—in tears.'

'She's a good little thing,' Harry said. 'I'm

very fond of her.'

'I didn't believe the police when they told me about you.'

Harry said, 'I wouldn't have asked you to come if I'd known what was going to happen, but I didn't think the police were on to me.'

'Were you going to cut me in on the spoils?'

'I've never kept you out of anything, old man, yet,' He stood with his back to the door as the car swung upwards, and smiled back at Rollo Martins, who could remember him in just such an attitude in a secluded corner of the school quad, saying, 'I've learned a way to get out at night. It's absolutely safe. You are the only one I'm letting in on it.' For the first time Rollo Martins looked back through the years without admiration, as he thought: He's never grown up. Marlowe's devils wore squibs attached to their tails: evil was like Peter Pan—it carried with it the horrifying and horrible gift of eternal youth.

Martins said, 'Have you ever visited the children's hospital? Have you seen any of your victims?'

Harry took a look at the toy landscape below and came away from the door. 'I never feel quite safe in these things,' he said. He felt the back of the door with his hand, as though he were afraid that it might fly open and launch him into that iron-ribbed space. 'Victims?' he asked. 'Don't be melodramatic, Rollo. Look down there,' he went on, pointing through the window at the people moving like black flies at the base of the Wheel. 'Would you really feel any pity if one of those dots stopped moving—for ever? If I said you can have twenty thousand pounds for every dot that stops, would you really, old man, tell me to keep my money—without hesitation? Or would you calculate how many dots you could afford to spare? Free of income tax, old man. Free of income tax.' He gave his boyish conspiratorial smile. 'It's the only way to save nowadays.'

'Couldn't you have stuck to tyres?'

'Like Cooler? No, I've always been ambitious.'

'You are finished now. The police know everything.'

'But they can't catch me, Rollo, you'll see. I'll pop up again. You can't keep a good man down.'

The car swung to a standstill at the highest point of the curve and Harry turned his back and gazed out of the window. Martins thought: One good shove and I could break the glass, and he pictured the body falling, falling, through the iron struts, a piece of carrion dropping among the flies. He said, 'You know the police are planning to dig up your body. What will they find?'

'Harbin,' Harry replied with simplicity. He turned away from the window and said, 'Look at the sky.'

The car had reached the top of the Wheel and hung there motionless, while the stain of the sunset ran in streaks over the wrinkled papery sky beyond the black girders.

'Why did the Russians try to take Anna Schmidt?'

'She had false papers, old man.'

'Who told them?'

'The price of living in this zone, Rollo, is service. I have to give them a little information now and then.'

'I thought perhaps you were just trying to get her here—because she was your girl? Because you wanted her?'

Harry smiled. 'I haven't all that influence.'

'What would have happened to her?'

'Nothing very serious. She'd have been sent back to Hungary. There's nothing against her really. A year in a labour camp perhaps. She'd be infinitely better off in her own country than being pushed around by the British police.'

'She hasn't told them anything about you.'

'She's a good little thing,' Harry repeated with satisfaction and pride.

'She loves you.'

'Well, I gave her a good time while it lasted.'

'And I love her.'

'That's fine, old man. Be kind to her. She's worth it. I'm glad.' He gave the impression of having arranged everything to everybody's satisfaction. 'And you can help to keep her mouth shut. Not that she knows anything that matters.'

'I'd like to knock you through the window.'

'But you won't, old man. Our quarrels never last long. You remember that fearful one in the Monaco, when we swore we were through. I'd trust you anywhere, Rollo. Kurtz tried to persuade me not to come but I know you. Then he tried to persuade me to, well, arrange an accident. He told me it would be quite easy in this car.'

'Except that I'm the stronger man.'

'But I've got the gun. You don't think a bullet wound would show when you hit *that* ground?' Again the car began to move, sailing slowly down, until the flies were midgets, were recognisable human beings. 'What fools we are, Rollo, talking like this, as if I'd do that to you—or you to me.' He turned his back

136

and leaned his face against the glass. One thrust . . . 'How much do you earn a year with your Westerns, old man?'

'A thousand.'

'Taxed. I earn thirty thousand free. It's the fashion. In these days, old man, nobody thinks in terms of human beings. Governments don't, so why should we? They talk of the people and the proletariat, and I talk of the mugs. It's the same thing. They have their five-year plans and so have I.'

'You used to be a Catholic.'

'Oh, I still *believe*, old man. In God and mercy and all that. I'm not hurting anybody's soul by what I do. The dead are happier dead. They don't miss much here, poor devils,' he added with that odd touch of genuine pity, as the car reached the platform and the faces of the doomed-to-be-victims, the tired pleasure-hoping Sunday faces, peered in at them. 'I could cut you in, you know. It would be useful. I have no one left in the Inner City.'

'Except Cooler? And Winkler?'

'You really mustn't turn policeman, old man.' They passed out of the car and he put his hand again on Martins' elbow. 'That was a joke, I know you won't. Have you heard anything of old Bracer recently?'

'I had a card at Christmas.'

'Those were the days, old man. Those were the days. I've got to leave you here. We'll see each other sometime. If you are in a jam, you can always get me at Kurtz's.' He moved away and, turning, waved the hand he had had the tact not to offer: it was like the whole past moving off under a cloud. Martins suddenly called after him, 'Don't trust me, Harry,' but there was too great a distance now between them for the words to carry.

# CHAPTER FIFTEEN

'ANNA was at the theatre,' Martins told me, 'for the Sunday matinée. I had to see the whole dreary comedy through a second time. About a middle-aged composer and an infatuated girl and an understanding—a terribly understanding—wife. Anna acted very badly—she wasn't much of an actress at the best of times. I saw her afterwards in her dressing-room, but she was badly fussed. I think she thought I was going to make a serious pass at her all the time, and she didn't want a pass. I told her Harry was alive—I thought she'd be glad and that I would hate to see how glad she was, but she sat in front of her make-up mirror and let the tears streak the grease-paint and I wished afterwards that she had been glad. She looked awful and I loved her. Then I told her about my interview with Harry, but she wasn't really paying much attention because when I'd finished she said, "I wish he was dead."'

'He deserves to be.'

'I mean he would be safe then—from everybody.'

I asked Martins, 'Did you show her the

photographs I gave you—of the children?'

'Yes. I thought, it's got to be kill or cure this time. She's got to get Harry out of her system. I propped the pictures up among the pots of grease. She couldn't avoid seeing them. I said, "The police can't arrest Harry unless they get him into this zone, and we've got to help!"

'She said, "I thought he was your friend." I said, "He *was* my friend." She said, "I'll never help you to get Harry. I don't want to see him again, I don't want to hear his voice. I don't want to be touched by him, but I won't do a thing to harm him."

'I felt bitter—I don't know why, because after all I had done nothing for her. Even Harry had done more for her than I had. I said, "You want him still," as though I were accusing her of a crime. She said, "I don't want him, but he's in me. That's a fact—not like friendship. Why, when I have a love dream, he's always the man."'

I prodded Martins on when he hesitated. 'Yes?'

'Oh, I just got up and left her then. Now it's your turn to work on me. What do you want me to do?'

'I want to act quickly. You see, it was Harbin's body in the coffin, so we can pick up

Winkler and Cooler right away. Kurtz is out of our reach for the time being, and so is the driver. We'll put in a formal request to the Russians for permission to arrest Kurtz and Lime: it makes our files tidy. If we are going to use you as our decoy, your message must go to Lime straight away—not after you've hung around in this zone for twenty-four hours. As I see it, you were brought here for a grilling almost as soon as you got back into the Inner City; you heard then from me about Harbin; you put two and two together and you go and warn Cooler. We'll let Cooler slip for the sake of the bigger game—we have no evidence he was in on the penicillin racket. He'll escape into the second Bezirk to Kurtz, and Lime will know you've played the game. Three hours later you send a message that the police are after you: you are in hiding and must see him.'

'He won't come.'

'I'm not so sure. We'll choose our hiding place carefully—where he'll think there's a minimum of risk. It's worth trying. It would appeal to his pride and his sense of humour if he could scoop you out. And it would stop your mouth.'

Martins said, 'He never used to scoop me out—at school.' It was obvious that he had

141

been reviewing the past with care and coming to conclusions.

'That wasn't such serious trouble and there was no danger of your squealing.'

He said, 'I told Harry not to trust me, but he didn't hear.'

'Do you agree?'

He had given me back the photographs of the children and they lay on my desk. I could see him take a long look at them. 'Yes,' he said, 'I agree.'

# CHAPTER SIXTEEN

ALL the first arrangements went according to plan. We delayed arresting Winkler, who had returned from the second Bezirk, until after Cooler had been warned. Martins enjoyed his short interview with Cooler. Cooler greeted him without embarrassment and with considerable patronage. 'Why, Mr. Martins, it's good to see you. Sit down. I'm glad everything went off all right between you and Colonel Calloway. A very straight chap, Calloway.'

'It didn't,' Martins said.

'You don't bear any ill-will, I'm sure, about my letting him know about you seeing Koch. The way I figured it was this—if you were innocent you'd clear yourself right away, and if you were guilty, well, the fact that I liked you oughtn't to stand in the way. A citizen has his duties.'

'Like giving false evidence at an inquest.'

Cooler said, 'Oh, that old story. I'm afraid you are riled at me, Mr. Martins. Look at it this way—you as a citizen, owing allegiance—'

'The police have dug up the body. They'll be after you and Winkler. I want you to warn

Harry . . .'

'I don't understand.'

'Oh, yes, you do.' And it was obvious that he did. Martins left him abruptly. He wanted no more of that kindly humanitarian face.

It only remained then to bait the trap. After studying the map of the sewer system I came to the conclusion that a café anywhere near the main entrance of the great sewer, which was placed in what Martins had mistakenly called a newspaper kiosk, would be the most likely spot to tempt Lime. He had only to rise once again through the ground, walk fifty yards, bring Martins back with him, and sink again into the obscurity of the sewers. He had no idea that this method of evasion was known to us: he probably knew that one patrol of the sewer police ended before midnight, and the next did not start till two, and so at midnight Martins sat in the little cold café in sight of the kiosk, drinking coffee after coffee. I had lent him a revolver; I had men posted as close to the kiosk as I could, and the sewer police were ready when zero hour struck to close the manholes and start sweeping the sewers inwards from the edge of the city. But I intended, if I could, to catch him before he went underground again. It would save trouble—and risk to Martins. So there, as I say, in the café Martins sat.

The wind had risen again, but it had brought no snow; it came icily off the Danube and in the little grassy square by the café it whipped up the snow like the surf on top of a wave. There was no heating in the café, and Martins sat warming each hand in turn on a cup of ersatz coffee—innumerable cups. There was usually one of my men in the café with him, but I changed them every twenty minutes or so irregularly. More than an hour passed. Martins had long given up hope and so had I, where I waited at the end of a phone several streets away, with a party of the sewer police ready to go down if it became necessary. We were luckier than Martins because we were warm in our great boots up to the thighs and our reefer jackets. One man had a small searchlight about half as big again as a car headlight strapped to his breast, and another man carried a brace of Roman candles. The telephone rang. It was Martins. He said, 'I'm perishing with cold. It's a quarter past one. Is there any point in going on with this?'

'You shouldn't telephone. You must stay in sight.'

'I've drunk seven cups of this filthy coffee. My stomach won't stand much more.'

145

'He can't delay much longer if he's coming. He won't want to run into the two o'clock patrol. Stick it another quarter of an hour, but keep away from the telephone.'

Martins' voice said suddenly, 'Christ, he's here! He's—' and then the telephone went dead. I said to my assistant, 'Give the signal to guard all manholes,' and to my sewer police, 'We are going down.'

What had happened was this. Martins was still on the telephone to me when Harry Lime came into the café. I don't know what he heard, if he heard anything. The mere sight of a man wanted by the police and without friends in Vienna speaking on the telephone would have been enough to warn him. He was out of the café again before Martins had put down the receiver. It was one of those rare moments when none of my men was in the café. One had just left and another was on the pavement about to come in. Harry Lime brushed by him and made for the kiosk. Martins came out of the café and saw my men. If he had called out then it would have been an easy shot, but it was not, I suppose, Lime the penicillin racketeer who was escaping down the street; it was Harry. He hesitated just long enough for Lime to put the kiosk between them; then he called out. 'That's him,' but

Lime had already gone to ground.

What a strange world unknown to most of us lies under our feet: we live above a cavernous land of waterfalls and rushing rivers, where tides ebb and flow as in the world above. If you have ever read the adventures of Allan Quatermain and the account of his voyage along the underground river to the city of Milosis, you will be able to picture the scene of Lime's last stand. The main sewer, half as wide as the Thames, rushes by under a huge arch, fed by tributary streams: these streams have fallen in waterfalls from higher levels and have been purified in their fall, so that only in these side channels is the air foul. The main stream smells sweet and fresh with a faint tang of ozone, and everywhere in the darkness is the sound of falling and rushing water. It was just past high tide when Martins and the policeman reached the river: first the curving iron staircase, then a short passage so low they had to stoop, and then the shallow edge of the water lapped at their feet. My man shone his torch along the edge of the current and said, 'He's gone that way,' for just as a deep stream when it shallows at the rim leaves an accumulation of debris, so the sewer left in the quiet water against the wall a scum of orange peel, old cigarette cartons, and the

147

like, and in this scum Lime had left his trail as unmistakably as if he had walked in mud. My policeman shone his torch ahead with his left hand, and carried his gun in his right. He said to Martins, 'Keep behind me, sir, the bastard may shoot.'

'Then why the hell should you be in front?'

'It's my job, sir.' The water came half-way up their legs as they walked; the policeman kept his torch pointing down and ahead at the disturbed trail at the sewer's edge. He said, 'The silly thing is the bastard doesn't stand a chance. The manholes are all guarded and we've cordoned off the way into the Russian zone. All our chaps have to do now is to sweep inwards down the side passages from the manholes.' He took a whistle out of his pocket and blew, and very far away, here and again there, came the notes of a reply. He said, 'They are all down here now. The sewer police, I mean. They know this place just as I know the Tottenham Court Road. I wish my old woman could see me now,' he said, lifting his torch for a moment to shine it ahead, and at that moment the shot came. The torch flew out of his hand and fell in the stream. He said, 'God blast the bastard!'

'Are you hurt?'

'Scraped my hand, that's all. A week off

work. Here, take this other torch, sir, while I tie my hand up. Don't shine it. He's in one of the side passages.' For a long time the sound of the shot went on reverberating: when the last echo died a whistle blew ahead of them, and Martins' companion blew an answer.

Martins said, 'It's an odd thing—I don't even know your name.'

'Bates, sir.' He gave a low laugh in the darkness. 'This isn't my usual beat. Do you know the Horseshoe, sir?'

'Yes.'

'And the Duke of Grafton?'

'Yes.'

'Well, it takes a lot to make a world.'

Martins said, 'Let me come in front. I don't think he'll shoot at me, and I want to talk to him.'

'I had orders to look after you, sir, careful.'

'That's all right.' He edged round Bates, plunging a foot deeper in the stream as he went. When he was in front he called out, 'Harry,' and the name sent up an echo, 'Harry, Harry, Harry!' that travelled down the stream and woke a whole chorus of whistles in the darkness. He called again, 'Harry. Come out. It's no use.'

A voice startlingly close made them hug the wall. 'Is that you, old man?' it called. 'What do you want me to do?'

'Come out. And put your hands above your head.'

'I haven't a torch, old man. I can't see a thing.'

'Be careful, sir,' Bates said.

'Get flat against the wall. He won't shoot at me,' Martins said. He called, 'Harry, I'm going to shine the torch. Play fair and come out. You haven't got a chance.' He flashed the torch on, and twenty feet away, at the edge of the light and the water, Harry stepped into view. 'Hands above the head, Harry.' Harry raised his hand and fired. The shot ricocheted against the wall a foot from Martins' head, and he heard Bates cry out. At the same moment a searchlight from fifty yards away lit the whole channel, caught Harry in its beams, Martins, the staring eyes of Bates slumped at the water's edge with the sewage washing to his waist. An empty cigarette carton wedged into his armpit and stayed. My party had reached the scene.

Martins stood dithering there above Bates' body, with Harry Lime halfway between us. We couldn't shoot for fear of hitting Martins, and the light of the searchlight dazzled Lime. We moved slowly on, our revolvers trained for a chance, and Lime turned this way and that way like a rabbit dazzled by headlights; then suddenly he took a flying jump into the deep central rushing stream. When we turned the searchlight after him he was submerged, and the current of the sewer carried him rapidly on, past the body of Bates, out of the range of the searchlight into the dark. What makes a man, without hope, cling to a few more minutes of existence? Is it a good quality or a bad one? I have no idea.

Martins stood at the outer edge of the searchlight beam, staring downstream. He had his gun in his hand now, and he was the only one of us who could fire with safety. I thought I saw a movement and called out to him, 'There. There. Shoot.' He lifted his gun and fired, just as he had fired at the same command all those years ago on Brinkworth Common, fired, as he did then, inaccurately. A cry of pain came tearing back like calico down the cavern: a reproach, an entreaty. 'Well done,' I called and halted by Bates' body. He was dead. His eyes remained blankly open as we turned the searchlight on him; somebody stooped and dislodged the carton and threw it in the river, which whirled it on—a scrap of yellow Gold Flake: he was certainly a long way from the Tottenham Court Road.

I looked up and Martins was out of sight in the darkness. I called his name and it was lost in a confusion of echoes, in the rush and the roar of the underground river. Then I heard a third shot.

Martins told me later, 'I walked upstream to find Harry, but I must have missed him in the dark. I was afraid to lift the torch: I didn't want to tempt him to shoot again. He must have been struck by my bullet just at the entrance of a side passage. Then I suppose he crawled up the passage to the foot of the iron stairs. Thirty feet above his head was the manhole, but he wouldn't have had the strength to lift it, and even if he had succeeded the police were waiting above. He must have known all that, but he was in great pain, and just as an animal creeps into the dark to die, so I suppose a man makes for the light. He wants to die at home, and the darkness is never home to *us*. He began to pull himself up the stairs, but then the pain took him and he couldn't go on. What made him whistle that absurd scrap of tune I'd been fool enough to believe he had written himself? Was he trying to attract attention, did he want a friend with him, even the friend who had trapped him, or was he delirious and had he no purpose at all? Anyway I heard his

152

whistle and came back along the edge of the stream, and felt the wall end and found my way up the passage where he lay. I said, "Harry," and the whistling stopped, just above my head. I put my hand on an iron handrail and climbed. I was still afraid he might shoot. Then, only three steps up, my foot stamped down on his hand, and he was there. I shone my torch on him: he hadn't got a gun; he must have dropped it when my bullet hit him. For a moment I thought he was dead, but then he whimpered with pain. I said, "Harry," and he swivelled his eyes with a great effort to my face. He was trying to speak, and I bent down to listen. "Bloody fool," he said—that was all. I don't know whether he meant that for himself—some sort of act of contrition, however inadequate (he was a Catholic)—or was it for me—with my thousand a year taxed and my imaginary cattle rustlers who couldn't even shoot a rabbit clean? Then he began to whimper again. I couldn't bear it any more and I put a bullet through him.'

'We'll forget that bit,' I said.

Martins said, 'I never shall.'

# CHAPTER SEVENTEEN

A THAW set in that night, and all over Vienna the snow melted, and the ugly ruins came to light again; steel rods hanging like stalactites, and rusty girders thrusting like bones through the grey slush. Burials were much simpler than they had been a week before when electric drills had been needed to break the frozen ground. It was almost as warm as a spring day when Harry Lime had his second funeral. I was glad to get him under earth again, but it had taken two men's deaths. The group by the grave was smaller now: Kurtz wasn't there, nor Winkler—only the girl and Rollo Martins and myself. And there weren't any tears.

After it was over the girl walked away without a word to either of us down the long avenue of trees that led to the main entrance and the tram stop, splashing through the melted snow. I said to Martins, 'I've got transport. Can I give you a lift?'

'No,' he said, 'I'll take a tram back.'

'You win, you've proved me a bloody fool.'

'I haven't won,' he said. 'I've lost.' I watched him striding off on his overgrown legs after the girl. He caught her up and they walked side by side. I don't think he said a word to her: it was like the end of a story except that before they turned out of my sight her hand was through his arm—which is how a story usually begins. He was a very bad shot and a very bad judge of character, but he had a way with Westerns (a trick of tension) and with girls (I wouldn't know what). And Crabbin? Oh, Crabbin is still arguing with the British Cultural Relations Society about Dexter's expenses. They say they can't pass simultaneous payments in Stockholm and Vienna. Poor Crabbin. Poor all of us, when you come to think of it.

# THE FALLEN IDOL

# PREFACE

*The Fallen Idol* unlike *The Third Man* was not written for the films. That is only one of many reasons why I prefer it. It was published as *The Basement Room* in 1935 and conceived on a cargo steamer on the way home from Liberia to relieve the tedium of the voyage. *The Fallen Idol* is, of course, a meaningless title for the original story printed here, and even for the film it always reminded me of the problem paintings of John Collier. It was chosen by the distributors.

I was surprised when Carol Reed suggested that I should collaborate with him on a film of *The Basement Room* because it seemed to me that the subject was unfilmable—a murder committed by the most sympathetic character and an unhappy ending which would certainly have imperilled the £250,000 that films nowadays cost.

However we went ahead, and in the conferences that ensued the story was quietly changed, so that the subject no longer concerned a small boy who unwittingly betrayed his best friend to the police, but dealt instead with a small boy who believed that his friend was a murderer and nearly procured his arrest by telling lies in his defence. I think this, especially with Reed's handling, was a good subject, but the reader must not be surprised by not finding it the subject of the original story.

Why was the scene changed to an Embassy? This was Reed's idea since we both felt that the large Belgravia house was already in these post-war years a period piece, and we did not want to make an historical film. I fought the solution for a while and then wholeheartedly concurred.

It is always difficult to remember which of us made which change in the original story except in certain details. For example the cross-examination of the girl beside the bed that she had used with Baines was mine: the witty interruption of the man who came to wind the clock was Reed's. The snake was mine (I have always liked snakes), and for a short while it met with Reed's sympathetic opposition.

Of one thing about both these films I have complete certainty, that their success is due to Carol Reed, the only director I know with that particular warmth of human sympathy, the extraordinary feeling for the right face for the right part, the exactitude of cutting, and

not least important the power of sympathis-
ing with an author's worries and an ability to
guide him.

# CHAPTER ONE

WHEN the front door had shut them out and the butler Baines had turned back into the dark heavy hall, Philip began to live. He stood in front of the nursery door, listening until he heard the engine of the taxi die out along the street. His parents were gone for a fortnight's holiday; he was 'between nurses', one dismissed and the other not arrived; he was alone in the great Belgravia house with Baines and Mrs. Baines.

He could go anywhere, even through the green baize door to the pantry or down the stairs to the basement living-room. He felt a stranger in his home because he could go into any room and all the rooms were empty.

You could only guess who had once occupied them: the rack of pipes in the smoking-room beside the elephant tusks, the carved wood tobacco jar; in the bedroom the pink hangings and pale perfumes and the three-quarter-finished jars of cream which Mrs. Baines had not yet cleared away; the high glaze on the never-opened piano in the drawing-room, the china clock, the silly little tables and the silver: but here Mrs. Baines

162

was already busy, pulling down the curtains, covering the chairs in dust-sheets.

'Be off out of here, Master Philip,' and she looked at him with her hateful peevish eyes, while she moved round, getting everything in order, meticulous and loveless and doing her duty.

Philip Lane went downstairs and pushed at the baize door; he looked into the pantry, but Baines was not there; then he set foot for the first time on the stairs to the basement. Again he had the sense: this is life. All his seven nursery years vibrated with the strange, the new experience. His crowded busy brain was like a city which feels the earth tremble at a distant earthquake shock. He was apprehensive, but he was happier than he had ever been. Everything was more important than before.

Baines was reading a newspaper in his shirt-sleeves. He said, 'Come in, Phil, and make yourself at home. Wait a moment and I'll do the honours,' and going to a white cleaned cupboard he brought out a bottle of ginger-beer and half a Dundee cake. 'Half-past eleven in the morning,' Baines said. 'It's opening time, my boy,' and he cut the cake and poured out the ginger-beer. He was more genial than Philip had ever known him, more at his ease, a man in his own home.

'Shall I call Mrs. Baines?' Philip asked, and he was glad when Baines said no. She was busy. She liked to be busy, so why interfere with her pleasure?

'A spot of drink at half-past eleven,' Baines said, pouring himself out a glass of ginger-beer, 'gives an appetite for chop and does no man any harm.'

'A chop?' Philip asked.

'Old Coasters,' Baines said, 'call all food chop.'

'But it's not a chop?'

'Well, it might be, you know, cooked with palm oil. And then some paw-paw to follow.'

Philip looked out of the basement window at the dry stone yard, the ash-can and the legs going up and down beyond the railings.

'Was it hot there?'

'Ah, you never felt such heat. Not a nice heat, mind, like you get in the park on a day like this. Wet,' Baines said, 'corruption.' He cut himself a slice of cake. 'Smelling of rot,' Baines said, rolling his eyes round the small basement room, from clean cupboard to clean cupboard, the sense of bareness, of nowhere to hide a man's secrets. With an air of regret for something lost he took a long draught of ginger-beer.

'Why did father live out there?'

164

'It was his job,' Baines said, 'same as this is mine now. And it was mine then too. It was a man's job. You wouldn't believe it now, but I've had forty niggers under me, doing what I told them to.'

'Why did you leave?'

'I married Mrs. Baines.'

Philip took the slice of Dundee cake in his hand and munched it round the room. He felt very old, independent and judicial; he was aware that Baines was talking to him as man to man. He never called him Master Philip as Mrs. Baines did, who was servile when she was not authoritative.

Baines had seen the world; he had seen beyond the railings, beyond the tired legs of typists, the Pimlico parade to and from Victoria. He sat there over his ginger pop with the resigned dignity of an exile; Baines didn't complain; he had chosen his fate; and if his fate was Mrs. Baines he had only himself to blame.

But to-day, because the house was almost empty and Mrs. Baines was upstairs and there was nothing to do, he allowed himself a little acidity.

'I'd go back tomorrow if I had the chance.'

'Did you ever shoot a nigger?'

'I never had any call to shoot,' Baines said.

'Of course I carried a gun. But you didn't need to treat them bad. That just made them stupid. Why,' Baines said, bowing his thin grey hair with embarrassment over the ginger pop, 'I loved some of those damned niggers. I couldn't help loving them. There they'd be laughing, holding hands; they liked to touch each other; it made them feel fine to know the other fellow was round. It didn't mean anything we could understand; two of them would go about all day without losing hold, grown men; but it wasn't love; it didn't mean anything we could understand.'

'Eating between meals,' Mrs. Baines said 'What would your mother say, Master Philip?'

She came down the steep stairs to the basement, her hands full of pots of cream and salve, tubes of grease and paste. 'You oughtn't to encourage him, Baines,' she said, sitting down in a wicker armchair and screwing up her small ill-humoured eyes at the Coty lipstick, Pond's cream, the Leichner rouge and Cyclax powder and Elizabeth Arden astringent.

She threw them one by one into the wastepaper basket. She saved only the cold cream. 'Telling the boy stories,' she said. 'Go along to the nursery, Master Philip, while I get lunch.'

Philip climbed the stairs to the baize door. He heard Mrs. Baines's voice like the voice in a nightmare when the small Price light has guttered in the saucer and the curtains move; it was sharp and shrill and full of malice, louder than people ought to speak, exposed.

'Sick to death of your ways, Baines, spoiling the boy. Time you did some work about the house,' but he couldn't hear what Baines said in reply. He pushed open the baize door, came up like a small earth animal in his grey flannel shorts into a wash of sunlight on a parquet floor, the gleam of mirrors dusted and polished and beautified by Mrs. Baines.

Something broke downstairs, and Philip sadly mounted the stairs to the nursery. He pitied Baines; it occurred to him how happily they could live together in the empty house if Mrs. Baines were called away. He didn't want to play with his Meccano sets; he wouldn't take out his train or his soldiers; he sat at the table with his chin on his hands: this is life; and suddenly he felt responsible for Baines, as if he were the master of the house and Baines an ageing servant who deserved to be cared for. There was not much one could do; he decided at least to be good.

He was not surprised when Mrs. Baines was agreeable at lunch; he was used to her changes. Now it was 'another helping of meat, Master Philip,' or 'Master Philip, a little more of this nice pudding.' It was a pudding he liked, Queen's pudding with a perfect meringue, but he wouldn't eat a second helping lest she might count that a victory. She was the kind of woman who thought that any injustice could be counterbalanced by something good to eat.

She was sour, but she liked making sweet things; one never had to complain of a lack of jam or plums; she ate well herself and added soft sugar to the meringue and the strawberry jam. The half light through the basement window set the motes moving above her pale hair like dust as she sifted the sugar, and Baines crouched over his plate saying nothing.

Again Philip felt responsibility. Baines had looked forward to this, and Baines was disappointed: everything was being spoilt. The sensation of disappointment was one which Philip could share; knowing nothing of love or jealousy or passion he could understand better than anyone this grief, something hoped for not happening, something promised not fulfilled, something exciting turning dull. 'Baines,' he said, 'will you take me for a walk this afternoon?'

'No,' Mrs. Baines said, 'no. That he won't. Not with all the silver to clean.'

'There's a fortnight to do it in,' Baines said.

'Work first, pleasure afterwards.' Mrs. Baines helped herself to some more meringue.

Baines suddenly put down his spoon and fork and pushed his plate away. 'Blast,' he said.

'Temper,' Mrs. Baines said softly, 'temper. Don't you go breaking any more things, Baines, and I won't have you swearing in front of the boy. Master Philip, if you've finished you can get down.' She skinned the rest of the meringue off the pudding.

'I want to go for a walk,' Philip said.

'You'll go and have a rest.'

'I will go for a walk.'

'Master Philip,' Mrs. Baines said. She got up from the table leaving her meringue unfinished, and came towards him, thin, menacing, dusty in the basement room. 'Master Philip, you do as you're told.' She took him by the arm and squeezed it gently; she watched him with a joyless passionate glitter and above her head the feet of the typists trudged back to the Victoria offices after the lunch interval.

'Why shouldn't I go for a walk?' But he weakened; he was scared and ashamed of being scared. This was life; a strange passion he couldn't understand moving in the basement room. He saw a small pile of broken glass swept into a corner by a waste-paper basket. He looked to Baines for help and only intercepted hate; the sad hopeless hate of something behind bars.

'Why shouldn't I?' he repeated.

'Master Philip,' Mrs. Baines said, 'you've got to do as you're told. You mustn't think just because your father's away, there's nobody here to—'

'You wouldn't dare,' Philip cried, and was startled by Baines's low interjection:

'There's nothing she wouldn't dare.'

'I hate you,' Philip said to Mrs. Baines. He pulled away from her and ran to the door, but she was there before him; she was old, but she was quick.

'Master Philip,' she said, 'you'll say you're sorry.' She stood in front of the door quivering with excitement. 'What would your father do if he heard you say that?'

She put a hand out to seize him, dry and white with constant soda, the nails cut to the quick, but he backed away and put the table between them, and suddenly to his surprise she smiled; she became again as servile as she had been arrogant. 'Get along with you, Master Philip,' she said with glee, 'I see I'm

170

going to have my hands full till your father and mother come back.'

She left the door unguarded and when he passed her she slapped him playfully. 'I've got too much to do to-day to trouble about you. I haven't covered half the chairs,' and suddenly even the upper part of the house became unbearable to him as he thought of Mrs. Baines moving about shrouding the sofas, laying out the dust-sheets.

So he wouldn't go upstairs to get his cap but walked straight out across the shining hall into the street, and again, as he looked this way and that way, it was life he was in the middle of.

# CHAPTER TWO

IT WAS the pink sugar cakes in the window on a paper doily, the ham, the slab of mauve sausage, the wasps driving like small torpedoes across the pane that caught Philip's attention. His feet were tired by pavements; he had been afraid to cross the road, had simply walked first in one direction, then in the other. He was nearly home now; the square was at the end of the street; this was a shabby outpost of Pimlico, and he smudged the pane with his nose looking for sweets, and saw between the cakes and ham a different Baines. He hardly recognised the bulbous eyes, the bald forehead. It was a happy, bold and buccaneering Baines, even though it was, when you looked closer, a desperate Baines.

Philip had never seen the girl. He remembered Baines had a niece and he thought that this might be her. She was thin and drawn, and she wore a white mackintosh; she meant nothing to Philip; she belonged to a world about which he knew nothing at all. He couldn't make up stories about her, as he could make them up about withered Sir Hubert Reed, the Permanent Secretary,

172

about Mrs. Wince-Dudley who came up once a year from Penstanley in Suffolk with a green umbrella and an enormous black hand-bag, as he could make them up about the upper servants in all the houses where he went to tea and games. She just didn't belong; he thought of mermaids and Undine; but she didn't belong there either, nor to the adventures of Emil, nor to the Bastables. She sat there looking at an iced pink cake in the detachment and mystery of the completely disinherited, looking at the half-used pots of powder which Baines had set out on the marble-topped table between them.

Baines was urging, hoping, entreating, commanding, and the girl looked at the tea and the china pots and cried. Baines passed his handkerchief across the table, but she wouldn't wipe her eyes; she screwed it in her palm and let the tears run down, wouldn't do anything, wouldn't speak, would only put up a silent despairing resistance to what she dreaded and wanted and refused to listen to at any price. The two brains battled over the tea-cups loving each other, and there came to Philip outside, beyond the ham and wasps and dusty Pimlico pane, a confused indication of the struggle.

He was inquisitive and he did not understand and he wanted to know. He went and stood in the doorway to see better; he was less sheltered than he had ever been; other people's lives for the first time touched and pressed and moulded. He would never escape that scene. In a week he had forgotten it; but it conditioned his career, the long austerity of his life; when he was dying he said: 'Who is she?'

Baines had won; he was cocky and the girl was happy. She wiped her face, she opened a pot of powder, and their fingers touched across the table. It occurred to Philip that it would be amusing to imitate Mrs. Baines's voice and call 'Baines' to him from the door.

It shrivelled them; you couldn't describe it in any other way; it made them smaller, they weren't happy any more and they weren't bold. Baines was the first to recover and trace the voice, but that didn't make things as they were. The sawdust was spilled out of the afternoon; nothing you did could mend it, and Philip was scared. 'I didn't mean . . .' He wanted to say that he loved Baines, that he had only wanted to laugh at Mrs. Baines. But he had discovered that you couldn't laugh at Mrs. Baines. She wasn't Sir Hubert Reed, who used steel nibs and carried a pen-wiper in his pocket; she wasn't Mrs. Wince-Dudley; she was darkness when the night-light went out in a draught; she was the frozen blocks of earth he had seen one winter in a graveyard when someone said, 'They need an electric drill'; she was the flowers gone bad and smelling in the little closet room at Penstanley. There was nothing to laugh about. You had to endure her when she was there and forget about her quickly when she was away, suppress the thought of her, ram it down deep.

Baines said, 'It's only Phil,' beckoned him in and gave him the pink iced cake the girl hadn't eaten, but the afternoon was broken, the cake was like dry bread in the throat. The girl left them at once; she even forgot to take the powder; like a small blunt icicle in her white mackintosh she stood in the doorway with her back to them, then melted into the afternoon.

'Who is she?' Philip asked. 'Is she your niece?'

'Oh, yes,' Baines said, 'that's who she is; she's my niece,' and poured the last drops of water on to the coarse black leaves in the teapot.

'May as well have another cup,' Baines said.

'The cup that cheers,' he said hopelessly,

175

watching the bitter black fluid drain out of the spout.

'Have a glass of ginger pop, Phil?'

'I'm sorry. I'm sorry, Baines.'

'It's not your fault, Phil. Why, I could believe it wasn't you at all, but her. She creeps in everywhere.' He fished two leaves out of his cup and laid them on the back of his hand, a thin soft flake, and a hard stalk. He beat them with his hand: 'To-day,' and the stalk detached itself, 'to-morrow, Wednesday, Thursday, Friday, Saturday, Sunday,' but the flake wouldn't come, stayed where it was, drying under his blows, with a resistance you wouldn't believe it to possess. 'The tough one wins,' Baines said.

He got up and paid the bill and out they went into the street. Baines said, 'I don't ask you to say what isn't true. But you needn't mention to Mrs. Baines you met us here.'

'Of course not,' Philip said, catching something of Sir Hubert Reed's manner, 'I understand, Baines.' But he didn't understand a thing; he was caught up in other people's darkness.

'It was stupid,' Baines said. 'So near home, but I hadn't got time to think, you see. I'd got to see her.'

'Of course, Baines.'

'I haven't time to spare,' Baines said. 'I'm not young. I've got to see that she's all right.'

'Of course you have, Baines.'

'Mrs. Baines will get it out of you if she can.'

'You can trust me, Baines,' Philip said in a dry important Reed voice; and then, 'Look out. She's at the window watching.' And there indeed she was, looking up at them, between the lace curtains, from the basement room, speculating. 'Need we go in, Baines?' Philip asked, cold lying heavy on his stomach like too much pudding; he clutched Baines's arm.

'Careful,' Baines said softly, 'careful.'

'But need we go in, Baines? It's early. Take me for a walk in the park.'

'Better not.'

'But I'm frightened, Baines.'

'You haven't any cause,' Baines said. 'Nothing's going to hurt you. You just run along upstairs to the nursery. I'll go down by the area and talk to Mrs. Baines.' But even he stood hesitating at the top of the stone steps pretending not to see her, where she watched between the curtains. 'In at the front door, Phil, and up the stairs.'

Philip didn't linger in the hall; he ran, slithering on the parquet Mrs. Baines had polished, to the stairs. Through the drawing-room doorway on the first floor he saw the draped chairs; even the china clock on the mantel was covered like a canary's cage; as he passed it, it chimed the hour, muffled and secret under the duster. On the nursery table he found his supper laid out: a glass of milk and a piece of bread and butter, a sweet biscuit, and a little cold Queen's pudding without the meringue. He had no appetite; he strained his ears for Mrs. Baines's coming, for the sound of voices, but the basement held its secrets; the green baize door shut off that world. He drank the milk and ate the biscuit, but he didn't touch the rest, and presently he could hear the soft precise footfalls of Mrs. Baines on the stairs: she was a good servant, she walked softly; she was a determined woman, she walked precisely.

But she wasn't angry when she came in; she was ingratiating as she opened the night-nursery door— 'Did you have a good walk, Master Philip?'—pulled down the blinds, laid out his pyjamas, came back to clear his supper. 'I'm glad Baines found you. Your mother wouldn't like you being out alone.' She examined the tray. 'Not much appetite, have you, Master Philip? Why don't you try a little of this nice pudding? I'll bring you up some more jam for it.'

'No, no, thank you, Mrs. Baines,' Philip said.

'You ought to eat more,' Mrs. Baines said. She sniffed round the room like a dog. 'You didn't take any pots out of the waste-paper basket in the kitchen, did you, Master Philip?'

'No,' Philip said.

'Of course you wouldn't. I just wanted to make sure.' She patted his shoulder and her fingers flashed to his lapel; she picked off a tiny crumb of pink sugar. 'Oh, Master Philip,' she said, 'that's why you haven't any appetite. You've been buying sweet cakes. That's not what your pocket money's for.'

'But I didn't,' Philip said. 'I didn't.'

She tasted the sugar with the tip of her tongue.

'Don't tell lies to me, Master Philip. I won't stand for it any more than your father would.'

'I didn't, I didn't,' Philip said. 'They gave it me. I mean Baines,' but she had pounced on the word 'they'. She had got what she wanted; there was no doubt about that, even when you didn't know what it was she wanted. Philip was angry and miserable and disappointed because he hadn't kept Baines's secret. Baines oughtn't to have trusted him; grown-up people should keep their own secrets, and yet here was Mrs. Baines immediately entrusting him with another.

'Let me tickle your palm and see if you can keep a secret.' But he put his hand behind him; he wouldn't be touched. 'It's a secret between us, Master Philip, that I know all about them. I suppose she was having tea with him,' she speculated.

'Why shouldn't she?' he said, the responsibility for Baines weighing on his spirit, the idea that he had got to keep her secret when he hadn't kept Baines's making him miserable with the unfairness of life. 'She was nice.'

'She was nice, was she?' Mrs. Baines said in a bitter voice he wasn't used to.

'And she's his niece.'

'So that's what he said,' Mrs. Baines struck softly back at him like the clock under the duster. She tried to be jocular. 'The old scoundrel. Don't tell him I know, Master Philip.' She stood very still between the table and the door, thinking very hard, planning something. 'Promise you won't tell. I'll give you that Meccano set, Master Philip. . . .'

He turned his back on her; he wouldn't promise, but he wouldn't tell. He would have nothing to do with their secrets, the responsibilities they were determined to lay on him. He was only anxious to forget. He had received already a larger dose of life than he had bargained for, and he was scared. 'A 2A Meccano set, Master Philip.' He never opened his Meccano set again, never built anything, never created anything, died, the old dilettante, sixty years later with nothing to show rather than preserve the memory of Mrs. Baines's malicious voice saying good night, her soft determined footfalls on the stairs to the basement, going down, going down.

# CHAPTER THREE

THE sun poured in between the curtains and Baines was beating a tattoo on the water-can. 'Glory, glory,' Baines said. He sat down on the end of the bed and said, 'I beg to announce that Mrs. Baines has been called away. Her mother's dying. She won't be back till to-morrow.'

'Why did you wake me up so early?' Philip said. He watched Baines with uneasiness; he wasn't going to be drawn in; he'd learnt his lesson. It wasn't right for a man of Baines's age to be so merry. It made a grown person human in the same way that you were human. For if a grown-up could behave so childishly, you were liable too to find yourself in their world. It was enough that it came at you in dreams: the witch at the corner, the man with a knife. So 'It's very early,' he complained, even though he loved Baines, even though he couldn't help being glad that Baines was happy. He was divided by the fear and the at-traction of life.

'I want to make this a long day,' Baines said. 'This is the best time.' He pulled the cur-tains back. 'It's a bit misty. The cat's been out all night. There she is, sniffing round the area. They haven't taken in any milk at 59. Emma's shaking out the mats at 63.' He said, 'This was what I used to think about on the Coast: somebody shaking mats and the cat coming home. I can see it to-day,' Baines said, 'just as if I was still in Africa. Most days you don't notice what you've got. It's a good life if you don't weaken.' He put a penny on the washstand. 'When you've dressed, Phil, run and get a *Mail* from the barrow at the corner. I'll be cooking the sausages.'

'Sausages?'

'Sausages,' Baines said. 'We're going to celebrate to-day. A fair bust.' He celebrated at breakfast, restless, cracking jokes, unaccountably merry and nervous. It was going to be a long long day, he kept on coming back to that: for years he had waited for a long day, he had sweated in the damp Coast heat, changed shirts, gone down with fever, lain between the blankets and sweated, all in the hope of this long day, that cat sniffing round the area, a bit of mist, the mats beaten at 63. He propped the *Mail* in front of the coffee-pot and read pieces aloud. He said, 'Cora Down's been married for the fourth time.' He was amused, but it wasn't his idea of a long day. His long day was the Park, watching the riders in the Row, seeing Sir Arthur Still-water pass beyond the rails ('He dined with us once in Bo; up from Freetown; he was governor there'), lunch at the Corner House for Philip's sake (he'd have preferred himself a glass of stout and some oysters at the York bar), the Zoo, the long bus ride home in the last summer light: the leaves in the Green Park were beginning to turn and the motors nuzzled out of Berkeley Street with the low sun gently glowing on their windscreens. Baines envied no one, not Cora Down, or Sir Arthur Stillwater, or Lord Sandale, who came out on to the steps of the Naval and Military and then went back again because he hadn't got anything to do and might as well look at another paper. 'I said don't let me see you touch that black again.' Baines had led a man's life; everyone on top of the bus pricked their ears when he told Philip all about it.

'Would you have shot him?' Philip asked, and Baines put his head back and tilted his dark respectable manservant's hat to a better angle as the bus swerved round the Artillery Memorial.

'I wouldn't have thought twice about it. I'd have shot to kill,' he boasted, and the bowed figure went by, steel helmet, the heavy cloak, the down-turned rifle and the folded hands.

'Have you got the revolver?'

'Of course I've got it,' Baines said. 'Don't I need it with all the burglaries there've been?' This was the Baines whom Philip loved: not Baines singing and carefree, but Baines responsible, Baines behind barriers, living this man's life.

All the buses streamed out from Victoria like a convoy of aeroplanes to bring Baines home with honour. 'Forty blacks under me,' and there waiting near the area steps was the proper conventional reward, love at lighting-up time.

'It's your niece,' Philip said, recognising the white mackintosh, but not the happy sleepy face. She frightened him like an unlucky number; he nearly told Baines what Mrs. Baines had said; but he didn't want to bother, he wanted to leave things alone.

'Why, so it is,' Baines said. 'I shouldn't wonder if she was going to have a bite of supper with us.' But he said they'd play a game, pretend they didn't know her, slip down the area steps, 'and here,' Baines said, 'we are,' lay the table, put out the cold sausages, a bottle of beer, a bottle of ginger pop, a flagon of harvest burgundy. 'Everyone his own drink,' Baines said. 'Run upstairs, Phil, and see if there's been a post.'

Philip didn't like the empty house at dusk before the lights went on. He hurried. He wanted to be back with Baines. The hall lay there in quiet and shadow prepared to show him something he didn't want to see. Some letters rustled down, and someone knocked. 'Open in the name of the Republic.' The tumbrils rolled, the head bobbed in the bloody basket. Knock, knock, and the postman's footsteps going away. Philip gathered the letters. The slit in the door was like the grating in a jeweller's window. He remembered the policeman he had seen peer through. He had said to his nurse, 'What's he doing?' and when she said, 'He's seeing if everything's all right,' his brain immediately filled with images of all that might be wrong. He ran to the baize door and the stairs. The girl was already there and Baines was kissing her. She leant breathless against the dresser. 'This is Emmy, Phil.'

'There's a letter for you, Baines.'

'Emmy,' Baines said, 'it's from her.' But he wouldn't open it. 'You bet she's coming back.'

'We'll have supper, anyway,' Emmy said. 'She can't harm that.'

'You don't know her,' Baines said. 'Nothing's safe. Damn it,' he said, 'I was a man once,' and he opened the letter.

'Can I start?' Philip asked, but Baines

186

didn't hear; he presented in his stillness and attention an example of the importance grown-up people attached to the written word: you had to write your thanks, not wait and speak them, as if letters couldn't lie. But Philip knew better than that, sprawling his thanks across a page to Aunt Alice who had given him a doll he was too old for. Letters could lie all right, but they made the lie permanent: they lay as evidence against you; they made you meaner than the spoken word.

'She's not coming back till to-morrow night,' Baines said. He opened the bottles, he pulled up the chairs, he kissed Emmy again against the dresser.

'You oughtn't to,' Emmy said, 'with the boy here.'

'He's got to learn,' Baines said, 'like the rest of us,' and he helped Philip to three sausages. He only took one for himself; he said he wasn't hungry; but when Emmy said she wasn't hungry either he stood over her and made her eat. He was timid and rough with her; he made her drink the Harvest Burgundy because he said she needed building up; he wouldn't take no for an answer, but when he touched her his hands were light and clumsy too, as if he were afraid to damage something delicate and didn't know how to handle anything so light.

'This is better than milk and biscuits, eh?'

'Yes,' Philip said, but he was scared, scared for Baines as much as for himself. He couldn't help wondering at every bite, at every draught of the ginger pop, what Mrs. Baines would say if she ever learnt of this meal; he couldn't imagine it, there was a depth of bitterness and rage in Mrs. Baines you couldn't sound. He said, 'She won't be coming back tonight?' but you could tell by the way they immediately understood him that she wasn't really away at all; she was there in the basement with them, driving them to longer drinks and louder talk, biding her time for the right cutting word. Baines wasn't really happy; he was only watching happiness from close to instead of from far away.

'No,' he said, 'she'll not be back till late tomorrow.' He couldn't keep his eyes off happiness; he'd played around as much as other men, he kept on reverting to the Coast as if to excuse himself for his innocence; he wouldn't have been so innocent if he'd lived his life in London, so innocent when it came to tenderness. 'If it was you, Emmy,' he said, looking at the white dresser, the scrubbed chairs, 'this'd be like a home.' Already the room was not quite so harsh; there was a little dust in corners, the silver needed a final polish, the morning's paper lay untidily on a chair. 'You'd better go to bed, Phil; it's been a long day.'

They didn't leave him to find his own way up through the dark shrouded house; they went with him, turning on lights, touching each other's fingers on the switches; floor after floor they drove the night back; they spoke softly among the covered chairs; they watched him undress, they didn't make him wash or clean his teeth, they saw him into bed and lit the night-light and left his door ajar. He could hear their voices on the stairs, friendly like the guests he heard at dinner-parties when they moved down to the hall, saying good night. They belonged; wherever they were they made a home. He heard a door open and a clock strike, he heard their voices for a long while, so that he felt they were not far away and he was safe. The voices didn't dwindle, they simply went out, and he could be sure that they were still somewhere not far from him, silent together in one of the many empty rooms, growing sleepy together as he grew sleepy after the long day.

He just had time to sigh faintly with satis-faction, because this too perhaps had been life, before he slept and the inevitable terrors of sleep came round him: a man with a tricolour hat beat at the door on His Majesty's service, a bleeding head lay on the kitchen table in a basket, and the Siberian wolves crept closer. He was bound hand and foot and couldn't move; they leapt around him breathing heavily; he opened his eyes and saw Mrs. Baines was there, her grey untidy hair in threads over his face, her black hat askew. A loose hairpin fell on the pillow and one musty thread brushed his mouth. 'Where are they?' she whispered. 'Where are they?'

# CHAPTER FOUR

PHILIP watched her in terror. Mrs. Baines was out of breath as if she had been searching all the empty rooms, looking under loose covers.

With her untidy grey hair and her black dress buttoned to her throat, her gloves of black cotton, she was so like the witches of his dreams that he didn't dare to speak. There was a stale smell in her breath.

'She's here,' Mrs. Baines said, 'you can't deny she's here.' Her face was simultaneously marked with cruelty and misery; she wanted to 'do things' to people, but she suffered all the time. It would have done her good to scream, but she daren't do that: it would warn them. She came ingratiatingly back to the bed where Philip lay rigid on his back and whispered, 'I haven't forgotten the Meccano set. You shall have it to-morrow, Master Philip. We've got secrets together, haven't we? Just tell me where they are.'

He couldn't speak. Fear held him as firmly as any nightmare. She said, 'Tell Mrs. Baines, Master Philip. You love your Mrs. Baines, don't you?' That was too much; he couldn't speak, but he could move his mouth in terrified denial, wince away from her dusty image.

She whispered, coming closer to him, 'Such deceit. I'll tell your father. I'll settle with you myself when I've found them. You'll smart; I'll see you smart.' Then immediately she was still, listening. A board had creaked on the floor below, and a moment later, while she stooped listening above his bed, there came the whispers of two people who were happy and sleepy together after a long day. The night-light stood beside the mirror and Mrs. Baines could see bitterly there her own reflection, misery and cruelty wavering in the glass, age and dust and nothing to hope for. She sobbed without tears, a dry, breathless sound; but her cruelty was a kind of pride which kept her going; it was her best quality, she would have been merely pitiable without it. She went out of the door on tiptoe, feeling her way across the landing, going so softly down the stairs that no one behind a shut door could hear her. Then there was complete silence again; Philip could move; he raised his knees; he sat up in bed; he wanted to die. It wasn't fair, the walls were down again between his world and theirs; but this time it was something worse than merriment that the grown people made him share; a passion moved in the house he recognised but could not understand.

It wasn't fair, but he owed Baines everything: the Zoo, the ginger pop, the bus ride home. Even the supper called on his loyalty. But he was frightened; he was touching something he touched in dreams: the bleeding head, the wolves, the knock, knock, knock. Life fell on him with savagery: you couldn't blame him if he never faced it again in sixty years. He got out of bed, carefully from habit put on his bedroom slippers, and tiptoed to the door: it wasn't quite dark on the landing below because the curtains had been taken down for the cleaners and the light from the street came in through the tall windows. Mrs. Baines had her hand on the glass door-knob; she was carefully turning it; he screamed, 'Baines, Baines.'

Mrs. Baines turned and saw him cowering in his pyjamas by the banisters; he was helpless, more helpless even than Baines, and cruelty grew at the sight of him and drove her up the stairs. The nightmare was on him again and he couldn't move; he hadn't any more courage left for ever; he'd spent it all, had been allowed no time to let it grow, no years of gradual hardening; he couldn't even scream.

But the first cry had brought Baines out of the best spare bedroom and he moved quicker than Mrs. Baines. She hadn't reached the top of the stairs before he'd caught her round the waist. She drove her black cotton gloves at his face and he bit her hand. He hadn't time to think, he fought her savagely like a stranger, but she fought back with knowledgeable hate. She was going to teach them all and it didn't really matter whom she began with; they had all deceived her; but the old image in the glass was by her side, telling her she must be dignified, she wasn't young enough to yield her dignity; she could beat his face, but she mustn't bite; she could push, but she mustn't kick.

Age and dust and nothing to hope for were her handicaps. She went over the banisters in a flurry of black clothes and fell into the hall; she lay before the front door like a sack of coals which should have gone down the area into the basement. Philip saw; Emmy saw; she sat down suddenly in the doorway of the best spare bedroom with her eyes open as if she were too tired to stand any longer. Baines went slowly down into the hall.

It wasn't hard for Philip to escape; they'd forgotten him completely; he went down the back, the servants' stairs, because Mrs.

Baines was in the hall; he didn't understand what she was doing lying there; like the startling pictures in a book no one had read to him, the things he didn't understand terrified him. The whole house had been turned over to the grown-up world; he wasn't safe in the night-nursery; their passions had flooded it. The only thing he could do was to get away, by the back stairs, and up through the area, and never come back. You didn't think of the cold, of the need of food and sleep; for an hour it would seem quite possible to escape from people for ever.

He was wearing pyjamas and bedroom slippers when he came up into the square, but there was no one to see him. It was that hour of the evening in a residential district when everyone is at the theatre or at home. He climbed over the iron railings into the little garden: the plane trees spread their large pale palms between him and the sky. It might have been an illimitable forest into which he had escaped. He crouched behind a trunk and the wolves retreated; it seemed to him between the little iron seat and the tree-trunk that no one would ever find him again. A kind of embittered happiness and self-pity made him cry; he was lost; there wouldn't be any more secrets to keep; he surrendered responsibility once and for all. Let grown-up people keep to their world and he would keep to his, safe in the small garden between the plane trees. 'In the lost childhood of Judas Christ was betrayed'; you could almost see the small unformed face hardening into the deep dilettante selfishness of age.

Presently the door of 48 opened and Baines looked this way and that; then he signalled with his hand and Emmy came; it was as if they were only just in time for a train, they hadn't a chance of saying good-bye; she went quickly by like a face at a window swept past the platform, pale and unhappy and not wanting to go. Baines went in again and shut the door; the light was lit in the basement, and a policeman walked round the square, looking into the areas. You could tell how many families were at home by the lights behind the first-floor curtains.

Philip explored the garden: it didn't take long: a twenty-yard square of bushes and plane-trees, two iron seats and a gravel path, a padlocked gate at either end, a scuffle of old leaves. But he couldn't stay: something stirred in the bushes and two illuminated eyes peered out at him like a Siberian wolf, and he thought how terrible it would be if Mrs. Baines found him there. He'd have no time to climb the railings; she'd seize him from behind.

He left the square at the unfashionable end and was immediately among the fish-and-chip shops, the little stationers selling Bagatelle, among the accommodation addresses and the dingy hotels with open doors. There were few people about because the pubs were open, but a blowsy woman carrying a parcel called out to him across the street and the commissionaire outside a cinema would have stopped him if he hadn't crossed the road. He went deeper: you could go farther and lose yourself more completely here than among the plane-trees. On the fringe of the square he was in danger of being stopped and taken back: it was obvious where he belonged: but as he went deeper he lost the marks of his origin. It was a warm night: any child in those free-living parts might be expected to play truant from bed. He found a kind of camaraderie even among grown-up people; he might have been a neighbour's child as he went quickly by, but they weren't going to tell on him, they'd been young once themselves. He picked up a protective coating of dust from the pavements, of smuts from the trains which passed along the backs in a spray of fire. Once he was caught in a knot of children running away from something or somebody, laughing as they ran; he was whirled with them round a turning and abandoned, with a sticky fruit-drop in his hand.

He couldn't have been more lost; but he hadn't the stamina to keep on. At first he feared that someone would stop him; after an hour he hoped that someone would. He couldn't find his way back, and in any case he was afraid of arriving home alone; he was afraid of Mrs. Baines, more afraid than he had ever been. Baines was his friend, but something had happened which gave Mrs. Baines all the power. He began to loiter on purpose to be noticed, but no one noticed him. Families were having a last breather on the doorsteps, the refuse bins had been put out and bits of cabbage stalks soiled his slippers. The air was full of voices, but he was cut off; these people were strangers and would always now be strangers; they were marked by Mrs. Baines and he shied away from them into a deep class-consciousness. He had been afraid of policemen, but now he wanted one to take him home; even Mrs. Baines could do nothing against a policeman. He sidled past a constable who was directing traffic, but he was too busy to pay him any attention. Philip sat down against a wall and cried.

It hadn't occurred to him that was the easiest way, that all you had to do was to surrender, to show you were beaten and accept kindness. . . . It was lavished on him at once by two women and a pawnbroker. Another policeman appeared, a young man with a sharp incredulous face. He looked as if he noted everything he saw in pocket-books and drew conclusions. A woman offered to see Philip home, but he didn't trust her: she wasn't a match for Mrs. Baines immobile in the hall. He wouldn't give his address; he said he was afraid to go home. He had his way; he got his protection. 'I'll take him to the station,' the policeman said, and holding him awkwardly by the hand (he wasn't married; he had his career to make) he led him round the corner up the stone stairs into the little bare over-heated room where Justice waited.

# CHAPTER FIVE

JUSTICE waited behind a wooden counter on a high stool; it wore a heavy moustache; it was kindly and had six children ('three of them nippers like yourself'); it wasn't really interested in Philip, but it pretended to be, it wrote the address down and sent a constable to fetch a glass of milk. But the young constable was interested; he had a nose for things.

'Your home's on the telephone, I suppose,' Justice said. 'We'll ring them up and say you are safe. They'll fetch you very soon. What's your name, sonny?'

'Philip.'

'Your other name.'

'I haven't got another name.' He didn't want to be fetched; he wanted to be taken home by someone who would impress even Mrs. Baines. The constable watched him, watched the way he drank the milk, watched him when he winced away from questions.

'What made you run away? Playing truant, eh?'

'I don't know.'

'You oughtn't to do it, young fellow. Think how anxious your father and mother will be.'

'They are away.'

'Well, your nurse.'

'I haven't got one.'

'Who looks after you, then?' That question went home. Philip saw Mrs. Baines coming up the stairs at him, the heap of black cotton in the hall. He began to cry.

'Now, now, now,' the sergeant said. He didn't know what to do; he wished his wife were with him; even a policewoman might have been useful.

'Don't you think it's funny,' the constable said, 'that there hasn't been an inquiry?'

'They think he's tucked up in bed.'

'You are scared, aren't you?' the constable said. 'What scared you?'

'I don't know.'

'Somebody hurt you?'

'No.'

'He's had bad dreams,' the sergeant said. 'Thought the house was on fire, I expect. I've brought up six of them. Rose is due back. She'll take him home.'

'I want to go home with you,' Philip said; he tried to smile at the constable, but the deceit was immature and unsuccessful.

'I'd better go,' the constable said. 'There may be something wrong.'

'Nonsense,' the sergeant said. 'It's a woman's job. Tact is what you need. Here's

Rose. Pull up your stockings, Rose. You're a disgrace to the Force. I've got a job of work for you.' Rose shambled in: black cotton stockings drooping over her boots, a gawky Girl Guide manner, a hoarse hostile voice. 'More tarts, I suppose.'

'No, you've got to see this young man home.' She looked at him owlishly.

'I won't go with her,' Philip said. He began to cry again. 'I don't like her.'

'More of that womanly charm, Rose,' the sergeant said. The telephone rang on his desk. He lifted the receiver. 'What? What's that?' he said. 'Number 48? You've got a doctor?' He put his hand over the telephone mouth. 'No wonder this nipper wasn't reported,' he said. 'They've been too busy. An accident. Woman slipped on the area stairs.'

'Serious?' the constable asked. The sergeant mouthed at him; you didn't mention the word death before a child (didn't he know? he had six of them), you made noises in the throat, you grimaced, a complicated shorthand for a word of only five letters anyway.

'You'd better go, after all,' he said, 'and make a report. The doctor's there.'

Rose shambled from the stove; pink apply-dapply cheeks, loose stockings. She stuck her hands behind her. Her large morgue-like mouth was full of blackened teeth. 'You told me to take him and now just because something interesting . . . I don't expect justice from a man . . .'

'Who's at the house?' the constable asked.

'The butler.'

'You don't think,' the constable said, 'he saw . . .'

'Trust me,' the sergeant said. 'I've brought up six. I know 'em through and through. You can't teach me anything about children.'

'He seemed scared about something.'

'Dreams,' the sergeant said.

'What name?'

'Baines.'

'This Mr. Baines,' the constable said to Philip, 'you like him, eh? He's good to you?' They were trying to get something out of him; he was suspicious of the whole roomful of them; he said 'yes' without conviction because he was afraid at any moment of more responsibilities, more secrets.

'And Mrs. Baines?'

'Yes.'

They consulted together by the desk. Rose was hoarsely aggrieved; she was like a female impersonator, she bore her womanhood with an unnatural emphasis even while she scorned it in her creased stockings and her weather-exposed face. The charcoal shifted in the stove; the room was over-heated in the mild late summer evening. A notice on the wall described a body found in the Thames, or rather the body's clothes: wool vest, wool pants, wool shirt with blue stripes, size ten boots, blue serge suit worn at the elbows, fifteen-and-a-half celluloid collar. They couldn't find anything to say about the body, except its measurements, it was just an ordinary body.

'Come along,' the constable said. He was interested, he was glad to be going, but he couldn't help being embarrassed by his company, a small boy in pyjamas. His nose smelt something, he didn't know what, but he smarted at the sight of the amusement they caused: the pubs had closed and the streets were full again of men making as long a day of it as they could. He hurried through the less frequented streets, chose the darker pavements, wouldn't loiter, and Philip wanted more and more to loiter, pulling at his hand, dragging with his feet. He dreaded the sight of Mrs. Baines waiting in the hall: he knew now that she was dead. The sergeant's mouthings had conveyed that; but she wasn't buried; she wasn't out of sight; he was going to see a dead person in the hall when the door opened.

The light was on in the basement, and to his relief the constable made for the area steps. Perhaps he wouldn't have to see Mrs. Baines at all. The constable knocked on the door because it was too dark to see the bell, and Baines answered. He stood there in the doorway of the neat bright basement room and you could see the sad complacent plausible sentence he had prepared wither at the sight of Philip; he hadn't expected Philip to return like that in the policeman's company. He had to begin thinking all over again; he wasn't a deceptive man; if it hadn't been for Emmy he would have been quite ready to let the truth lead him where it would.

'Mr. Baines?' the constable asked.

He nodded; he hadn't found the right words; he was daunted by the shrewd knowing face, the sudden appearance of Philip there.

'This little boy from here?'

'Yes,' Baines said. Philip could tell that there was a message he was trying to convey, but he shut his mind to it. He loved Baines, but Baines had involved him in secrets, in fears he didn't understand. The glowing morning thought 'This is life' had become under Baines's tuition the repugnant memory, 'That was life': the musty hair across the mouth, the breathless cruel tortured inquiry 'Where are they?', the heap of black cotton tipped into the hall. That was what happened when you loved: you got involved; and Philip extricated himself from life, from love, from Baines with a merciless egotism.

There had been things between them, but he laid them low, as a retreating army cuts the wires, destroys the bridges. In the abandoned country you may leave much that is dear—a morning in the Park, an ice at a Corner House, sausages for supper—but more is concerned in the retreat than temporary losses. There are old people who, as the tractors wheel away, implore to be taken, but you can't risk the rearguard for their sake: a whole prolonged retreat from life, from care, from human relationship is involved.

'The doctor's here,' Baines said. He nodded at the door, moistened his mouth, kept his eyes on Philip, begging for something like a dog you can't understand. 'There's nothing to be done. She slipped on those stone basement stairs. I was in here. I heard her fall.' He wouldn't look at the constable's spidery writing which got a terrible lot on one page.

'Did the boy see anything?'

'He can't have done. I thought he was in bed. Hadn't we better go up? It's a shocking thing. Oh,' Baines said, losing control, 'it's a shocking thing for a child.'

'She's through here?' the constable asked.

'I haven't moved her an inch,' Baines said.

'He'd better then—'

'Go up the area and through the hall,' Baines said and again he begged dumbly like a dog: one more secret, keep this secret, do this for old Baines, he won't ask another.

'Come along,' the constable said. 'I'll see you up to bed. You're a gentleman; you must come in the proper way through the front door like the master should. Or will you go along with him, Mr. Baines, while I see the doctor?'

'Yes,' Baines said, 'I'll go.' He came across the room to Philip, begging, begging, all the way with his soft old stupid expression: this is Baines, the old Coaster; what about a palm-oil chop, eh? a man's life; forty niggers; never used a gun; I tell you I couldn't help loving them: it wasn't what we call love, nothing we could understand. The messages flickered out from the last posts at the border, imploring, beseeching, reminding: this is your old friend Baines; what about an elevens; a glass of ginger-pop won't do you any harm; sausages;

a long day. But the wires were cut, the messages just faded out into the enormous vacancy of the neat scrubbed room in which there had never been a place where a man could hide his secrets.

'Come along, Phil, it's bedtime. We'll just go up the steps . . .' Tap, tap, tap, at the telegraph; you may get through, you can't tell, somebody may mend the right wire. 'And in at the front door.'

'No,' Philip said, 'no. I won't go. You can't make me go. I'll fight. I won't see her.'

The constable turned on them quickly. 'What's that? Why won't you *go*?'

'She's in the hall,' Philip said. 'I know she's in the hall. And she's dead. I won't see her.'

'You moved her then?' the constable said to Baines. 'All the way down here? You've been lying, eh? That means you had to tidy up. . . . Were you alone?'

'Emmy,' Philip said, 'Emmy.' He wasn't going to keep any more secrets: he was going to finish once and for all with everything, with Baines and Mrs. Baines and the grown-up life beyond him; it wasn't his business and never, never again, he decided, would he share their confidences and companionship. 'It was all Emmy's fault,' he protested with a quaver which reminded Baines that after all he was only a child; it had been hopeless to expect help there; he was a child; he didn't understand what it all meant; he couldn't read this shorthand of terror; he'd had a long day and he was tired out. You could see him dropping asleep where he stood against the dresser, dropping back into the comfortable nursery peace. You couldn't blame him. When he woke in the morning, he'd hardly remember a thing.

'Out with it,' the constable said, addressing Baines with professional ferocity, 'who is she?' just as the old man sixty years later startled his secretary, his only watcher, asking, 'Who is she? Who is she?' dropping lower and lower into death, passing on the way perhaps the image of Baines: Baines hopeless, Baines letting his head drop, Baines 'coming clean'.